MW01135000

Edited by
STEVE DAVIDSON
and
JEAN MARIE STINE

Amazing Stories Classics
Produced by Digital Parchment Services

ISBN 9781500715953

Produced by Digital Parchment Services
Book and Cover Design: Frankie Hill

Contents

INTRODUCTION

THIS is the first of a series of books reprinting the best stories and novelettes drawn from each year of *Amazing Stories*' illustrious past. This is a somewhat strange omission considering that by the 1950s the other top science fiction magazines, *Galaxy, Astounding (Analog)*, and *The Magazine of F&SF*, were all producing annual "best of" collections. Yet those are the years when *Amazing Stories* was at its peak, featuring authors like Heinlein, Asimov, Sturgeon, Bradbury, Clarke, Miller, Sheckley, Dick, Budrys, Bixby, Bloch, Leiber, Ellison, Silverberg, and others. But their loss is your gain because you are holding now the first edition of the first-ever such year-by-year "Best of Amazing Stories." We plan to be publishing a minimum of six such volumes each year. So watch for *The Best of Amazing Stories 1927*.

Many of the stories in this inaugural volume are recognized classics, like "The Man from the Atom," "The Eggs from Lake Tanganyika" and "The Runaway Skyscraper" (with its surprisingly modern handling). Others such as "Whispering Ether" and "The Telepathic Pick-Up" have been overlooked and never reprinted outside the pages of those debut 1926 issues of *Amazing Stories*. While each is of its time, affording a unique view into the prevailing mores, scientific ideas and stylistic approaches, every story is eminently readable and contains an intriguing storyline.

We at the new *Amazing Stories* are sure you will enjoy reading them as much as we did as we combed through the pages of those now moldering 1926 issues for the golden nuggets of entertainment and enlightenment they contain.

Steve Davidson
Jean Marie Stine

The MAN *from the* ATOM

By G. Peyton Wertenbaker

I looked down, and Professor Martyn, a tiny speck in an automobile far below, waved up to me cheerfully as he started his car and began to speed away. He was fleeing the immediate danger of my growth, when my feet would begin to cover an immense area, until I could be almost entirely in space.

Introduction

IN "Alice in Wonderland" the beautiful play of fancy which gave immortal fame to a logician and mathematician we read of the mysterious change in size of the heroine, the charming little Alice. It tells how she grew large and small according to what she ate. But here we have increase in size and pushed to its utmost limit. Here we have treated the growth of a man to cosmic dimensions. And we are told of his strange sensation and are led up to a sudden startling and impressive conclusion, and are taken through the picture of his emotions and despair.

THE MAN FROM THE ATOM

By G. Peyton Wertenbaker

CHAPTER I

I AM a lost soul, and I am homesick. Yes, homesick. Yet how vain is homesickness when one is without a home! I can but be sick for a home that has gone. For my home departed millions of years ago, and there is now not even a trace of its former existence. Millions of years ago, I say, in all truth and earnestness. But I must tell the tale—though there is no man left to understand it.

I well remember that morning when my friend, Professor Martyn, called me to him on a matter of the greatest importance. I may explain that the Professor was one of those mysterious outcasts, geniuses whom Science would not recognize because they scorned the pettiness of the men who represented Science. Martyn was first of all a scientist, but almost as equally he was a man of intense imagination, and where the ordinary man crept along from detail to detail and required a complete model before being able to visualize the results of his work, Professor Martyn first grasped the great results of his contemplated work, the vast, far-reaching effects, and then built with the end in view.

The Professor had few friends. Ordinary men avoided him because they were unable to understand the greatness of his vision. Where he plainly saw pictures of worlds and universes, they vainly groped among pictures of his words on printed pages. That was their impression of a word. A group of letters. His was of the picture it presented in his mind. I, however, though I had not the slightest claim to scientific knowledge, was romantic to a high degree, and always willing to carry out his strange experiments for the sake of the adventure and the strangeness of it all, And so the advantages were equal. I had a mysterious personage ready to furnish me with the unusual. He had a willing subject to try out his inventions, for he reasoned quite naturally that should he himself perform the experiments, the world would be in danger of losing a mentality it might eventually have need of.

And so it was that I hurried to him without the slightest hesitation upon that, to me, momentous day of days in my life. I little realized the great change that soon would come over my existence, yet I knew that I was in for an adventure, certainly startling, possibly fatal. I had no delusions concerning my luck.

I found Professor Martyn in his laboratory bending, with the eyes of a miser counting his gold, over a tiny machine that might easily have fitted in my pocket. He did not see me for a moment, but when he finally looked up with a sigh of regret that he must tear his eyes away from his new and wonderful brain-child, whatever it might be, he waved me a little unsteadily into a chair, and sank down in one himself, with the machine in his lap. I waited, placing myself in what I considered a receptive mood.

"Kirby," he began abruptly at last, "have you ever read your Alice in Wonderland?" I gasped, perhaps, in my surprise.

"Alice in—! are you joking, Professor?"

"Certainly not," he assured me. "I speak in all seriousness."

"Why, yes, I have read it many times. In fact, it has always struck me as a book to appeal more to an adult than to a child. But what—I can't see just how that is important." He smiled.

"Perhaps I am playing with you unduly," he said, "but do you remember the episode of the two pieces of cheese, if my own recollection is correct, one of which made one grow, the other shrink?"

I assented. "But," I said incredulously, "certainly you cannot tell me you have spent your time in preparing magical cheeses?" He laughed aloud this time, and then, seeing my discomfort, unburdened himself of his latest triumph.

"No Kirby, not just that, but I have indeed constructed a machine that you will be incapable of believing until you try it. With this little object in my lap, you could grow forever, until there was nothing left in the universe to surpass. Or you could shrink so as to observe the minutest of atoms, standing upon it as you now stand upon the earth. It is an invention that will make scientific knowledge perfect!" He halted with flushed face and gleaming eyes. I could find nothing to say, for the thing was collossal, magnificent in its possibilities. If it worked. But I could not resist a suspicion of so tiny a machine.

"Professor, are you in absolute earnest?" I cried.

"Have I ever jested about so wonderful a thing?" he retorted quietly. I knew he had not.

"But surely that is merely a model?"

"It is the machine itself!"

CHAPTER II

I WAS too astounded to speak at first. But finally, "Tell me about it," I gasped. "This is certainly the most fantastic invention you have made yet! How does it work?"

"I am afraid," suggested Professor Martyn, "that you could not understand all the technical details. It is horribly complicated. And besides, I am anxious to try it out. But I will give you an idea of it.

"Of course, you know that an object may be divided in half forever, as you have learned in high school, without being entirely exhausted. It is this principle that is used in shrinking. I hardly understand the thing's mechanism myself—it was the result of an accident—but I know that the machine not only divides every atom, every molecule, every electron of the body into two exactly equal parts, but it accomplishes the same feat in itself, thus keeping pace with its manipulator. The matter it removes from the body is reduced to a gaseous form, and left in the air. There are six wires that you do not see, which connect with the body, while the machine itself is placed on the chest, held by a small belt that carries wires to the front of the body where the two controlling buttons are placed.

"When the user wishes to grow, he presses the upper button, and the machine then extracts atoms from the air which it converts, by a reverse method from the first, into atoms identical to certain others in the body, the two atoms thus formed joining into one large particle of twice the original size.

"As I said, I have little idea of my invention except that it works by means of atomic energy. I was intending to make an atomic energy motor, when I observed certain parts to increase and diminish strangely in size. It was practically by blind instinct that I have worked the thing up. And now I fear I shall not be able to discover the source of my atomic energy until I can put together, with great care, another such machine, for I am afraid to risk taking this apart for analysis."

"And I," I said suddenly, with the awe I felt for such a discovery quite perceptible, I fear, in my tone, "I am to try out this machine?"

"If you are willing," he said simply. "You must realize, of course, that there are a multitude of unknown dangers. I know nothing of the complete effects of the machine. But my experiments on inanimate objects have seemed satisfactory."

"I am willing to take any risks," I said enthusiastically, "If you are willing to risk your great machine. Why, don't you realize, Professor, that this will revolutionize Science? There is nothing, hardly, that will be unknown. Astronomy will be complete, for there will be nothing to do but to increase in size enough to observe beyond our atmosphere, or one could stand upon worlds like rocks to examine others."

"Exactly. I have calculated that the effect of a huge foot covering whole countries would be slight, so equally distributed would the weights be. Probably it would rest upon tall buildings and trees with ease. But in space, of course, no support should be necessary.

"And then, as you said, one could shrink until the mysteries of electrons would be revealed. Of course, there would be danger in descending into apparent nothingness, not knowing where a new world-atom could be found upon which to stand. But dangers must be risked."

"But now, Kirby," remarked the Professor officially, "time passes, and I should like you to make your little journey soon that I may quickly know its results. Have you any affairs you would like to put in order, in case—"

"None," I said. I was always ready for these experiments. And though this promised to be magnificently momentous, I was all ready. "No, if I return in a few hours, I shall find everything all right. If not, I am still prepared." He beamed in approval.

"Fine. Of course you understand that our experiment must take place at some secluded spot. If you are ready, we can proceed at once to a country laboratory of mine that will, I think, be safe."

I assented, and we hastily donned our overcoats, the Professor spending a moment or two collecting some necessary apparatus. Then we packed the machine in a safe box, and left his home.

"Are you all ready, Kirby?" The Professor's voice was firm, but my practiced ear could detect the slightest vibrations that indicated to me his intense inner feelings. I hesitated a moment. I was not afraid of going. Never that. But there seemed something partaking almost of finality about this departure. It was different from anything I had ever felt before.

"All ready, Professor," I said cheerfully after a brief moment.

"Are you going to magnify or minimize yourself?"

"It shall be growth," I answered, without a moment's hesitation there. The stars, and what lay beyond... It was that

I cared for. The Professor looked at me earnestly, deeply engrossed in thought. Finally he said, "Kirby, if you are to make an excursion into interstellar space, you realize that not only would you freeze to death, but also die from lack of air."

Walking to a cabinet in the rear of the room, he opened it and withdrew from it some strange looking paraphernalia. "This," he said, holding up a queer looking suit, "is made of a great quantity of interlocking metal cells, hermetically sealed, from which the air has been completely exhausted so as to give the cells a high vacuum. These separate cells are then woven into the fabric. When you wear this suit, you will, in fact, be enclosed in a sort of thermos bottle. No heat can leave this suit, and the most intensive cold cannot penetrate through it."

I quickly got into the suit, which was not as heavy as one might imagine. It covered not only the entire body, but the feet and hands as well, the hand part being a sort of mitten.

After I had gotten into the suit, the Professor placed over my head a sort of transparent dome which he explained was made of strong unbreakable bakelite. The globe itself really was made of several globes, one within the other. The globes only touched at the lower rim. The interstices where the globes did not touch formed a vacuum, the air having been drawn from the spaces. Consequently heat could not escape from the transparent head piece nor could the cold come in. From the back of this head gear, a flexible tube led into the interior; this tube being connected to a small compressed oxygen tank, which the Professor strapped to my back.

He then placed the wonder machine with its row of buttons on my chest, and connected the six wires to the arms and other parts of my body.

Professor Martyn grasped my hand then, and said in his firm, quiet voice:

"Then goodbye, Kirby, for awhile. Press the first button when you are ready to go. May the Fates be with you!"

The Professor next placed the transparent head gear over my head and secured it with attachments to my vacuum suit. A strange feeling of quietness and solitude came over me. While I could still see the Professor, I could hear him talk no longer as sounds cannot pierce a vacuum. Once more the Professor shook my hand warmly.

Then, somehow, I found myself pressing down the uppermost of three buttons. Instantly there was a tingling, electric flash all through my body. Martyn, trees, distant buildings, all seemed to shoot away into nothingness. Almost in panic, I pushed the middle button. I stopped. I could not help it, for this disappearing of all my world acted upon my consciousness. I had a strange feeling that I was leaving forever.

I looked down; and Professor Martyn, a tiny speck in an automobile far below, waved up to me cheerfully as he started his car and began to speed away. He was fleeing the immediate danger of my growth, when my feet would begin to cover an immense area, until I could be almost entirely in space. I gathered my courage quickly, fiercely, and pressed the top button again. Once more the earth began to get smaller, little by little, but faster. A tingling sensation was all over me, exhilarating if almost painful where the wires were connected upon my forearms, my legs, about the forehead, and upon my chest.

It did never seem as though I was changing, but rather that the world was shrinking away, faster and faster. The clouds were falling upon me with threatening swiftness, until my head broke suddenly through them, and my body was obscured, and the earth below, save tiny glimpses, as though of a distant landscape through a fog. Far away I could see a few tall crags that broke through even as had I, scorning from their majestic height the world below. Now indeed, if never before, was my head "among the clouds!"

But even the clouds were going. I began to get an idea of the earth as a great ball of thick cloud. There was a pricking sensation beneath my feet, as though I stood upon pine needles. It gave me a feeling of power to know that these were trees and hills.

I began to feel insecure, as though my support were doing something stealthy beneath me. Have you ever seen an elephant perform upon a little rolling ball? Well that is how I felt. The earth was rotating, while I no longer could move upon it. While I pondered, watching in some alarm as it became more and more like a little ball a few feet thick, it took matters in its own hand. My feet slipped off, suddenly, and I was lying absolutely motionless, powerless to move, in space!

I watched the earth awhile as it shrank, and even observed it now as it moved about the sun. I could see other planets that had grown at first a trifle larger and were now getting smaller again, about the same size as the earth, tiny balls of no more than a couple of inches in diameter...

It was getting much darker. The sun no longer gave much light, for there was no atmosphere to diffuse it. It was a great blinding ball of fire near my feet now, and the planets were traveling about it swiftly. I could see the light reflected on one side, dark on the other, on each planet. The sun could be seen to move perceptibly too, though very slightly. As my feet grew larger, threatening to touch it, I hastily drew them up with ease and hung suspended in the sky in a half-sitting position as I grew.

Turning my head away all at once, I observed in some surprise that some of the stars were growing larger, coming nearer and nearer. For a time I watched their swift approach, but they gradually seemed to be getting smaller rather than larger. I looked again at my own system. To my amazement, it had moved what seemed about a yard from its former position, and was much smaller. The planets I saw no longer, but there were faint streaks of light in circles about the sun, and I understood that these were the tracks of the worlds that now moved about their parent too swiftly to be followed with the eye.

I could see all the stars moving hither and yon now, although they still continued to appear closer and closer together. I found a number lying practically on the plane of my chest, but above that they seemed to cease. I could now see no planets, only the tiny sun moving farther and farther, faster and faster along its path. I could discern, it seemed to me, a trend in its and its companions' path. For on one side they seemed to be going one way, and the opposite way on the other. In front, they seemed to move across my vision. Gradually I came to understand that this was a great circle swinging vastly about me, faster and faster.

I had grown until the stars were circling now about my legs. I seemed to be the center of a huge vortex. And they were coming closer and closer together, as though to hem me about. Yet I could not move all of me away. I could only move my limbs and head in relation to my stationary body. The nearest star, a tiny bright speck, was a few yards away. My own sun was like a bright period upon a blackboard. But the stars were coming nearer and nearer. It seemed necessary for me to move somehow, so I drew my legs up and shot them out with all my force. I began to move slowly away, having acted upon what little material substance there was in the ether.

The stars were soon only a few feet apart below me, then a few inches, and suddenly, looking out beyond them, I was struck with the fact that they seemed to be a great group, isolated from a number of far distant blotches that were apart from these. The stars were moving with incredible swiftness now about a center near which was what I imagined to be the sun, though I had lost track of it somehow. They merged closer and closer together, the vast group shrunk more and more, until finally they had become indistinguishable as entities. They were all part of a huge cloud now, that seemed somehow familiar. What did it suggest? It was pale, diffused at the ends, but thick and white in the center, like a nebul—a nebula! That was it! A great light broke over me. All these stars were part of a great system that formed a nebula. It explained the mystery of the nebulae.

And there were now other nebulae approaching, as this grew smaller. They took on the resemblance of stars, and they began to repeat the process of closing in as the stars had done. The stars, universes within universes! And those universes but nebulae in another great universe! Suddenly I began to wonder. Could there be nothing more in infinity than universe after universe, each a part of another greater one? So it would seem. Yet the spell was upon me and I was not ready to admit such simplicity yet. I must go on. And my earth! It could not even be found, this sphere that had itself seemed almost the universe.

But my growth was terribly fast now. The other nebulae were merging, it would seem at first, upon me. But my slow progress through space became faster as I grew larger, and even as they came upon me, like flying arrows now, I shot above them. Then they, too, merged. The result was a vast nucleus of glowing material.

A great light began to grow all about me. Above I suddenly observed, far away, a huge brightness that seemed to extend all over the universe. But it began definitely. It was as though one were in a great ball, and the nebulae, a sunlike body now, were in the center. But as I became larger with every instant, the roof-like thing diffused, even as before things had converged, and formed into separate bodies, like stars. I passed through them finally, and they came together again behind me as I shot away, another great body.

A coincidence suddenly struck me. Was not this system of a great ball effect with a nucleus within similar to what the atom was said to be? Could the nucleus and its great shell be opposite poles of electrical energy, then? In other words, was this an electron—a huge electron composed of universes? The idea was terrible in its magnitude, something too huge for comprehension.

And so I grew on. Many more of these electrons, if such they were, gathered together, but my luck held and I passed beyond this new body thus formed—a molecule? I wondered. Suddenly I tired of the endless procession of stars coming together, forming ever into new stars that came together too. I was getting homesick. I wanted to see human faces about me again, to be rid of this fantastic nightmare. It was unreal. It was impossible. It must stop.

A sudden impulse of fear took hold upon me. This should not go on forever. I had to see my earth again. All at once, I reached down, and pressed the central button to stop.

But just as a swiftly moving vehicle may not stop at once,

so could not I. The terrific momentum of my growth carried me on, and the machine moved still, though slower. The stars seemed shooting upon me, closing about me. I could see no end of them before me. I must stop or they would be about me.

Closer in they came, but smaller and smaller. They became a thousand pinpoints shooting about me. They merged into a thick, tenuous cloud about me, thicker and thicker. I was shooting up now, but my growth had stopped. The cloud became a cold, clammy thing that yielded to the touch, and—and it was water! Yes, pure water! And I was floating in it. . .

Years. . . .

Suddenly I shot up, out of the water, and fell back. Strength returned to me, and warmth, and love of life. It was water, something I knew, something familiar, a friend. And so I swam, swam on and on, until my feet touched bottom, and I was leaping forth out of the water, on to the sand. . . .

CHAPTER III

THERE is no need to drag the tale out. I awoke finally from an exhausted sleep, and found myself in a world that was strange, yet familiar. It might have been a lonely part of the earth, except for an atmosphere of strangeness that told me subconsciously it was another world. There was a sun, but it was far distant, no larger than my moon. And vast clouds of steam hung over the jungles beyond the sand, obscuring them in a shimmering fog, obscuring the sun so that it danced and glimmered hazily through the curtain. And a perpetual twilight thus reigned.

I tried to tell myself I was in some strange manner home. But I knew I was not. At last, breaking beneath the weight of homesickness and regret, I surrendered to a fit of weeping that shamed my manhood even as I wept. Then a mood of terrible, unreasoning anger against Fate enveloped me, and I stormed here and there about the beach.

And so, all through the night, I alternately wept and raged, and when the dawn came I sank again in peaceful slumber...

When I awoke, I was calm. Obviously, in stopping I told myself I had been left in a cloud of atoms that proved to be part of another group of matter, another earth or atom, as you will. The particular atoms I was in were part of the ocean.

The only thing to do was to return. I was ashamed of my madness now, for I had the means of return. In the third button…the bottom button. I saw no reason for delay. I splashed back into the water, and swam hastily out to the point where it seemed I had risen. I pushed the lowest button. Slowly I felt myself grow smaller and smaller, the sense of suffocation returned, only to pass away as the pinpoints shot about me again, but away this time. The whole nightmare was repeated now, reversed, for everything seemed to be opening up before me. I thrilled with joy as I thought of my return to my home, and the Professor again. All the world was friend to me now, in my thoughts, a friend I could not bear to lose.

And then all my hopes were dashed. How, I thought, could I strike my own earth again? For even if I had come to the right spot in the water to a certainty, how could I be sure I would pass between just the right cloud of molecules? And what would lead me to the very electron I had left? And, after the nucleus, why should I not enter the wrong nebula? And even if I should hit the right nebula, how should I find my own star, my own earth? It was hopeless, impossible!… And yet, so constituted is human nature that I could hope nevertheless!

My God! Impossible as it is, I did it! I am certain that it was my own nebula I entered, and I was in the center, where the sun should be. It sounds fantastic, it *is* fantastic. The luck of a lifetime, an infinity, for me. Or so it should have been. But I looked where the sun ought to be found, in the central cluster. I halted early and watched long with a sinking heart. But the sun—was gone!

I lay motionless in the depths of space and I watched idly the stars that roamed here and there. Black despair was in my heart, but it was a despair so terrible that 1 could not comprehend its awfulness. It was beyond human emotion. And I was dazed, perhaps even a little mad.

The stars were tiny pinpoints of light, and they shot back and forth and all around like purposeless nothings. And ever would they collide, and a greater pinpoint would be born, or a thousand pieces of fragments would result. Or the two might start off on new tracks, only to collide again. Seconds it took them to cover what I knew to be billions of trillions of light-years.

And gradually the truth dawned upon me, the awful truth. These stars were suns, even as mine had been, and they grew and died and were reborn, it seemed now, in a second, all in a second. Yet fair races bloomed and died, and worlds lived and died, races of intelligent beings strove, only to die. All in a second. But it was not a second to them. My immense size was to blame on my part.

For time is relative, and depends upon size. The smaller a creature, the shorter its life. And yet, to itself, the fly that lives but a day has passed a lifetime of years. So it was here. Because I had grown large, centuries had become but moments to me. And the faster, the larger I grew, the swifter the years, the millions of years had rolled away. I remembered how I had seen the streaks that meant the planets going about the sun. So fast had they revolved that I could not see the circuit that meant but a second to me. And yet each incredibly swift revolution had been a year! A year on earth, a second to me! And so, on an immensely greater scale, had it been as I grew. The few minutes that meant to me the sun's movement through the ether of what seemed a yard had been centuries to the earth. Before I had lived ten minutes of my strange existence, Professor Martyn had vainly hoped away a lifetime, and died in bitter despair. Men had come and died, races had flourished and fallen. Perhaps all mankind had died away from a world stripped of air and water. In ten minutes of my life...

And so I sit here now, pining hopelessly for my Mother Earth. This strange planet of a strange star is all beyond my ken. The men are strange and their customs, curious. Their language is beyond my every effort to comprehend, yet mine they know like a book. I find myself a savage, a creature to be treated with pity and contempt in a world too advanced even for his comprehension. Nothing here means anything to me.

I live here on sufferance, as an ignorant African might have lived in an incomprehensible, to him, London. A strange creature, to play with and to be played with by children. A clown...a savage...! And yearn as I will for my earth, I know I may never know it again, for it was gone, forgotten, non-existent a trillion centuries ago!

The MAN WHO SAVED *the* EARTH

By Austin Hall

Not a sound; the whole works a complicated mass covering a hundred acres, driving with a silence that was magic. Not a whir nor friction. Like a living composite body pulsing and breathing the strange and mysterious force that had been evolved from Huyck's theory of kinetics. The four great steel conduits running from the globes down the side of the mountain. In the center, at a point midway between the globes, a massive steel needle hung on a pivot and pointed directly at the sun.

Introduction

WE read of the days when the powers of radium were yet unknown. It is told us that burns were produced by incautiously carrying a tube of radium salts in the pocket. And here in this story we are told of a different power, opalescence, due to another element. It can destroy mountains, excavate cavities of immeasurable depths and kill human beings and animals in multitude. The story opens with a poor little boy experimenting with a burning glass. Then he becomes the hero of the story—he studies and eventually finds himself able to destroy the earth. He exceeds Archimedes in his power. And he suddenly finds that he has unlocked a power that threatens this very destruction. And the story depicts his horror at the Frankenstein which he had unloosed, and tells of his wild efforts to save humanity, and of the loss of the cosmic discoveries of the little newsboy grown up to be a great scientist.

THE MAN WHO SAVED THE EARTH

By Austin Hall

CHAPTER I
The Beginning

EVEN the beginning. From the start the whole thing has the precision of machine work. Fate and its working—and the wonderful Providence which watches over Man and his future. The whole thing unerring:

the incident, the work, the calamity, and the martyr. In the retrospect of disaster we may all of us grow strong in wisdom. Let us go into history.

A hot July day. A sun of scant pity, and a staggering street; panting thousands dragging along, hatless; fans and parasols; the sultry vengeance of a real day of summer. A day of bursting tires; hot pavements, and wrecked endeavor, heartaches for the seashore, for leafy bowers beside rippling water, a day of broken hopes and listless ambition.

Perhaps Fate chose the day because of its heat and because of its natural benefit on fecundity. We have no way of knowing. But we do know this: the date, the time, the meeting; the boy with the burning glass and the old doctor. So commonplace, so trivial and hidden in obscurity! Who would have guessed it? Yet it is—after the creation—one of the most important dates in the world's history.

This is saying a whole lot. Let us go into it and see what it amounts to. Let us trace the thing out in history, weigh it up and balance it with sequence.

Of Charley Huyck we know nothing up to this day. It is a thing which, for some reason, he has always kept hidden. Recent investigation as to his previous life and antecedents have availed us nothing. Perhaps he could have told us; but as he has gone down as the world's great martyr, there is no hope of gaining from his lips what we would so like to know.

After all, it does not matter. We have the day—the incident, and its purport, and its climax of sequence to the day of the great disaster. Also we have the blasted mountains and the lake of blue water which will ever live with his memory. His greatness is not of warfare, nor personal ambition; but of all mankind. The wreaths that we bestow upon him have no doubtful color. The man who saved the earth!

From such a beginning, Charley Huyck, lean and frail of body, with, even then, the wistfulness of the idealist, and the eyes of a poet. Charley Huyck, the boy, crossing the hot pavement with his pack of papers; the much treasured piece of glass in his pocket, and the sun which only he should master burning down upon him. A moment out of the ages; the turning of a straw destined to out-balance all the previous accumulation of man's history.

The sun was hot and burning, and the child—he could not have been more than ten—cast a glance over his shoulder. It was in the way of calculation. In the heyday of childhood he was not dragged down by the heat and weather: he had the enthusiasm of his half-score of years and the joy of the plaything. We will not presume to call it the spirit of the scientist, though it was, perhaps, the spark of latent investigation that was destined to lead so far.

A moment picked out of destiny! A boy and a plaything. Uncounted millions of boys have played with glass and the sun rays. Who cannot remember the little, round-burning dot in the palm of the hand and the subsequent exclamation? Charley Huyck had found a new toy, it was a simple thing and as old as glass. Fate will ever be so in her working.

And the doctor? Why should he have been waiting? If it was not destiny, it was at least an accumulation of moment. In the heavy eye-glasses, the square, close-cut beard; and his uncompromising fact-seeking expression. Those who knew Dr. Robold are strong in the affirmation that he was the antithesis of all emotion. He was the sternest product of science: unbending, hardened by experiment, and caustic in his condemnation of the frailness of human nature.

It had been his one function to topple over the castles of the foolish; with his hard-seeing wisdom he had spotted sophistry where we thought it not. Even into the castles of science he had gone like a juggernaut. It is hard to have one's theories derided— yea, even for a scientist—and to be called a fool! Dr. Robold knew no middle language; he was not relished by science.

His memory, as we have it, is that of an eccentric. A man of slight compassion, abrupt of manner and with no tact in speaking. Genius is often so; it is a strange fact that many of the greatest of men have been denied by their follows. A great man and laughter. He was not accepted.

None of us know today what it cost Dr. Robold. He was not the man to tell us. Perhaps Charley Huyck might; but his lips are sealed forever. We only know that he retired to the mountain, and of the subsequent flood of benefits that rained upon mankind. And we still denied him. The great cynic on the mountain. Of the secrets of the place we know little. He was not the man to accept the investigator; he despised the curious. He had been laughed at—let be—he would work alone on the great moment of the future.

In the light of the past we may well bend knee to the doctor and his protégé, Charley Huyck. Two men and destiny! What would we be without them? One shudders to think. A little thing, and yet one of the greatest moments in the world's history. It must have been Fate, Why was it that this stern man, who hated all emotion, should so have unbended at this moment? That we cannot answer. But we can conjecture. Mayhap it is this: We were all wrong; we accepted the man's exterior and profession as the fact of his marrow.

No man can lose all emotion. The doctor, was, after all, even as ourselves—he was human. Whatever may be said, we have the certainty of that moment—and of Charley Huyck.

The sun's rays were hot; they were burning; the pavements

were intolerable; the baked air in the canyoned street was dancing like that of an oven; a day of dog-days. The boy crossing the street; his arms full of papers, and the glass bulging in his little hip-pocket.

At the curb he stopped. With such a sun it was impossible to long forget his plaything. He drew it carefully out of his pocket, lay down a paper and began distancing his glass for the focus. He did not notice the man beside him. Why should he? The round dot, the brownish smoke, the red spark and the flash of flame! He stamped upon it. A moment out of boyhood; an experimental miracle as old as the age of glass, and just as delightful. The boy had spoiled the name of a great Governor of a great State; but the paper was still salable. He had had his moment. Mark that moment.

A hand touched his shoulder. The lad leaped up.

"Yessir. *Star* or *Bulletin*?"

"I'll take one of each," said the man. "There now. I was just watching you. Do you know what you were doing?"

"Yessir. Burning paper. Startin' fire. That's the way the Indians did it."

The man smiled at the perversion of fact. There is not such a distance between sticks and glass in the age of childhood.

"I know," he said—"the Indians. But do you know how it was done; the why—why the paper began to blaze?"

"Yessir."

"All right, explain."

The boy looked up at him. He was a city boy and used to the streets. Here was some old highbrow challenging his wisdom. Of course he knew.

"It's the sun."

"There," laughed the man. "Of course. You said you knew, but you don't. Why doesn't the sun, without the glass, burn the paper? Tell me that."

The boy was still looking up at him; he saw that the man was not like the others on the street. It may be that the strange intimacy kindled into being at that moment. Certainly it was a strange unbending for the doctor.

"It would if it was hot enough or you could get enough of it together."

"Ah! Then that is whet the glass is for, is it?"

"Yessir."

"Concentration?"

"Con—— I don't know, sir. But it's the sun. She's sure some hot. I know a lot about the sun, sir. I've studied it with the glass. The glass picks up all the rays and puts them in one hole and that's what burns the paper.

"It's lots of fun. I'd like to have a bigger one; but it's all I've got. Why, do you know, if I had a glass big enough and a place to stand, I'd burn up the earth?"

The old man laughed. "Why, Archimides! I thought you were dead."

"My name ain't Archimedes. It's Charley Huyck."

Again the old man laughed.

"Oh, is it? Well, that's a good name, too. And if you keep on you'll make it famous as the name of the other." Wherein he was foretelling history. "Where do you live?"

The boy was still looking. Ordinarily he would not have told, but he motioned back with his thumb.

"I don't live; I room over on Brennan Street."

"Oh, I see. You room. Where's your mother?"

"Search me; I never saw her."

"I see; and your father?"

"How do I know. He went floating when I was four years old."

"Floating?"

"Yessir—to sea."

"So your mother's gone and your father's floating. Archimedes is adrift. You go to school?"

"Yessir."

"What reader?"

"No reader. Sixth grade.

"I see. What school?"

"School Twenty-six. Say, it's hot. I can't stand here all day. I've got to sell my papers."

The man pulled out a purse.

"I'll take the lot," he said. Then kindly: "My boy, I would like to have you go with me."

It was a strange moment. A little thing with the fates looking on. When destiny plays she picks strange moments. This was one. Charley Huyck went with Dr. Robold.

CHAPTER II
The Poison Pall

WE all of us remember that fatal day when the news startled all of Oakland. No one can forget it. At first it read like a newspaper hoax, in spite of the oft-proclaimed veracity of the press, and we were inclined to laughter. 'Twixt wonder at the story and its impossibilities we were not a little enthused at the nerve of the man who put it over.

It was in the days of dry reading. The world had grown populous and of well-fed content. Our soap-box artists had come to the point at last where they preached, not disaster, but a full-bellied thanks for the millennium that was here. A period of Utopian quietness—no villain around the corner; no man to covet the ox of his neighbor.

Quiet reading, you'll admit. Those were the days of the millennium. Nothing ever happened. Here's hoping they never come again. And then:

Honestly, we were not to blame for bestowing blessing out of our hearts upon that newspaperman. Even if it were a hoax, it was at least something.

At high noon. The clock in the city hall had just struck the hour that held the post 'twixt a.m. and p.m., a hot day with a sky that was clear and azure; a quiet day of serene peace and contentment. A strange and a portent moment. Looking back and over the miracle we may conjecture that it was the clearness of the atmosphere and the brightness of the sun that helped to the impact of the disaster. Knowing what we know now we can appreciate the impulse of natural phenomena. It was *not* a miracle.

The spot: Fourteenth and Broadway, Oakland, California.

Fortunately the thousands of employees in the stores about had not yet come out for their luncheons. The lapse that it takes to put a hat on, or to pat a ribbon, saved a thousand lives. One shudders to think of what would have happened had the spot been crowded. Even so, it was too impossible and too terrible to be true. Such things could not happen.

At high noon: Two street-cars crossing Fourteenth on Broadway—two cars with the-same joggle and bump and the same aspect of any of a hundred thousand at a traffic corner. The wonder is—there were so few people. A Telegraph car outgoing, and a Broadway car coming in. The traffic policeman at his post had just given his signal. Two automobiles were passing and a single pedestrian, so it is said, was working his way diagonally across the corner. Of this we are not certain.

It was a moment that impinged on miracle. Even as we recount it, knowing, as we do, the explanation, we sense the impossibility of the event. A phenomenon that holds out and, in spite of our findings, lingers into the miraculous. To be and not to be. One moment life and action, an ordinary scene of existent monotony; and the next moment nothing. The spot, the intersection of the street, the passing street-cars, the two automobiles, pedestrian, the policeman—non-existent! When events are instantaneous reports are apt to be misleading. This is what we find.

Some of those who beheld it, report a flash of bluish white light; others that it was of a greenish or even a violet hue; and others, no doubt of stronger vision, that it was not only of a predominant color but that it was shot and sparkled with a myriad specks of flame and burning.

It gave no warning and it made no sound; not even a whir. Like a hot breath out of the void. Whatever the forces that had focused, they were destruction. There was no Fourteenth and Broadway. The two automobiles, the two street-cars, the pedestrian, the policeman had been whiffed away as if they had never existed. In place of the intersection of the thoroughfares was a yawning gulf that looked down into the center of the earth to a depth of nausea.

It was instantaneous; it was without sound; no warning. A tremendous force of unlimited potentiality had been loosed to kinetic violence. It was the suddenness and the silence that belied credence. We were accustomed to associate all disaster with confusion; calamity has an affinity with pandemonium, all things of terror climax into sound. In this case there was no sound. Hence the wonder.

A hole or bore forty feet in diameter. Without a particle of warning and without a bit of confusion. The spectators one and all aver that at first they took it for nothing more than the effect of startled eyesight. Almost subtle. It was not until after a full minute's reflection that they became aware that a miracle had been wrought before their faces. Then the crowd rushed up and with awe and now awakened terror gazed down into that terrible pit.

We say "terrible" because in this case it is an exact adjective. The strangest hole that man ever looked into. It was so deep that at first it appeared to have no bottom; not even the strongest eyesight could penetrate the smoldering blackness that shrouded the depths descending. It took a stout heart and courage to stand and hold one's head on the brink for even a minute.

It was straight and precipitous; a perfect circle in shape; with sides as smooth as the effect of machine work, the pavement and stone curb had been cut as if by a razor. Of the two street cars, two automobiles and their occupants there was nothing. The whole thing so silent and complete. Not even the spectators could really believe it.

It was a hard thing to believe. The newspapers themselves, when the news came clamoring, accepted it with reluctance. It was too much like a hoax. Not until the most trusted reporters had gone and had wired in their reports would they even consider it. Then the whole world sat up and took notice.

A miracle! Like Oakland's *Press* we all of us doubted that hole. We had attained almost everything that was worth the knowing; we were the masters of the earth and its secrets and we were proud of our wisdom; naturally we refused such reports all out of reason. It must be a hoax.

But the wires were persistent. Came corroboration. A reliable news-gathering organization soon was coming through with elaborate and detailed accounts of just what was happening. We had the news from the highest and most reputable authority.

And still we doubted. It was the story itself that brought the doubting; its touch on miracle. It was too easy to pick on the reporter. There might be a hole, and all that; but this thing of no explanation! A bomb perhaps? No noise? Some new explosive? No such thing? Well, how did we know? It was better than a miracle.

Then came the scientists. As soon as could be men of great minds had been hustled to the scene. The world had long been accustomed to accept without quibble the dictum of these great specialists of fact. With their train of accomplishments behind them we would hardly be consistent were we to doubt them.

We know the scientist and his habits. He is the one man who will believe nothing until it is proved. It is his profession, and for that we pay him. He can catch the smallest bug that ever crawled out of an atom and give it a name so long that a Polish wrestler, if he had to bear it, would break under the burden. It is his very knack of getting in under that has given us our civilization. You don't baffle a scientist in our Utopia. It can't be done. Which is one of the very reasons why we began to believe in the miracle.

In a few moments a crowd of many thousands had gathered about the spot; the throng grew so dense that there was peril of some of them being crowded into the pit at the center. It took all the spare policemen of the city to beat them back far enough to string ropes from the corners. For blocks the streets were packed with wondering thousands. Street traffic was impossible. It was necessary to divert the cars to a roundabout route to keep the arteries open to the suburbs.

Wild rumors spread over the city. No one knew how many

passengers had been upon the street cars. The officials of the company, from the schedule, could pick the numbers of the cars and their crews; but who could tell of the occupants?

Telephones rang with tearful pleadings. When the first rumors of the horror leaked out every wife and mother felt the clutch of panic at her heartstrings. It was a moment of historical psychology. Out of our books we had read of this strange phase of human nature that was wont to rise like a mad screeching thing out of disaster. We had never had it in Utopia.

It was rumbling at first and out of exaggeration; as the tale passed farther back to the waiting thousands it gained with the repetition. Grim and terrible enough in fact, it ratioed up with reiteration. Perhaps after all it was not psychology. The average impulse of the human mind does not even up so exactly. In the light of what we now know it may have been the poison that had leaked into the air; the new element that was permeating the atmosphere of the city.

At first it was spasmodic. The nearest witnesses of the disaster were the first victims. A strange malady began to spot out among those of the crowd who had been at the spot of contact. This is to be noticed. A strange affliction which from the virulence and rapidity of action was quite puzzling to the doctors.

Those among the physicians who would consent to statement gave it out that it was breaking down of tissue. Which of course it was; the new element that was radiating through the atmosphere of the city. They did not know it then.

The pity of it! The subtle, odorless pall was silently shrouding out over the city. In a short time the hospitals were full and it was necessary to call in medical aid from San

Francisco. They had not even time for diagnosis. The new plague was fatal almost at conception. Happily the scientists made the discovery.

It was the pall. At the end of three hours it was known that the death sheet was spreading out over Oakland. We may thank our stars that it was learned so early. Had the real warning come a few hours later the death list would have been appalling.

A new element had been discovered; or if not a new element, at least something which was tipping over all the laws of the atmospheric envelope. A new combination that was fatal. When the news and the warning went out, panic fell upon the bay shore.

But some men stuck. In the face of such terror there were those who stayed and with grimness and sacrifice hung to their posts for mankind. There are some who had said that the stuff of heroes had passed away. Let them then consider the case of John Robinson.

Robinson was a telegraph operator. Until that day he was a poor unknown; not a whit better than his fellows. Now he has a name that will run in history. In the face of what he knew he remained under the blanket. The last words out of Oakland—his last message:

"Whole city of Oakland in grip of strange madness. Keep out of Oakland,"—following which came a haphazard personal commentary:

"I can feel it coming on myself. It is like what our ancestors must have felt when they were getting drunk—alternating desires of fight and singing—a strange sensation, light, and ecstatic with a spasmodic twitching over the forehead. Terribly thirsty. Will stick it out if I can get enough water. Never so dry in my life."

Followed a lapse of silence. Then the last words:

"I guess we're done for. There is some poison in the atmosphere—something. It has leaked, of course, out of this thing at Fourteenth and Broadway. Dr. Manson of the American Institute says it is something new that is forming a fatal combination; but he cannot understand a new element; the quantity is too enormous.

"Populace has been warned out of the city. All roads are packed with refugees. The Berkeley Hills are covered as with flies—north, east, and south and on the boats to Frisco. The poison, whatever it is, is advancing in a ring from Fourteenth and Broadway. You have got to pass it to these old boys of science. They are staying with that ring. Already they have calculated the rate of its advance and have given warning. They don't know what it is, but they have figured just how fast it is moving. They have saved the city.

"I am one of the few men now inside the wave. Out of curiosity I have stuck. I have a jug and as long as it lasts I shall stay. Strange feeling. Dry, dry, dry, as if the juice of one's life cells was turning into dust. Water evaporating almost instantly. It cannot pass through glass. Whatever the poison it has an affinity for moisture. Do not understand it. I have had enough—"

That was all. After that there was no more news out of Oakland. It is the only word that we have out of the pall itself. It was short and disconnected and a bit slangy; but for all that a basis from which to conjecture.

It is a strange and glorious thing how some men will stick to the post of danger. This operator knew that it meant death; but he held with duty. Had he been a man of scientific training his information might have been of incalculable value. However, may God bless his heroic soul!

What we know is thirst! The word that came from the experts confirmed it. Some new element of force was stealing or sapping the humidity out of the atmosphere. Whether this was combining and entering into a poison could not be determined.

Chemists worked frantically at the outposts of the advancing ring. In four hours it had covered the city; in six it had reached San Leandro, and was advancing on toward Haywards.

It was a strange story and incredible from the beginning. No wonder the world doubted. Such a thing had never happened. We had accepted the the law of judging the future by the past; by deduction; we were used to sequence and to law; to the laws of Nature. This thing did look like a miracle; which was merely because—as usually it is with "miracles"—we could not understand it. Happily, we can look back now and still place our faith in Nature.

The world doubted and was afraid. Was this peril to spread slowly over the whole state of California and then on to the—world. Doubt always precedes terror. A tense world waited. Then came the word of reassurance—from the scientists:

"Danger past; vigor of the ring is abating. Calculation has deduced that the wave is slowly decreasing in potentiality. It is too early yet to say that there will be recessions, as the wave is just reaching its zenith. What it is we cannot say; but it cannot be inexplicable. After a little time it will all be explained. Say to the world there is no cause for alarm."

But the world was now aroused; as it doubted the truth before, it doubted now the reassurance. Did the scientists know? Could they have only seen the future! We know now that they did not. There was but one man in all the world great enough to foresee disaster. That man was Charley Huyck.

CHAPTER III
The Mountain That Was

ON the same day on which all this happened, a young man, Pizzozi by name and of Italian parentage, left the little town of Ione in Amador County, California, with a small truck-load of salt. He was one of the cattlemen whose headquarters or home-farms are clustered about the foot-bills of the Sierras. In the wet season they stay with their home-land in the valley; in the summer they penetrate into the mountains. Pizzozi had driven in from the mountains the night before, after salt. He had been on the road since midnight.

Two thousand salt-hungry cattle do not allow time for gossip. With the thrift of his race, Joe had loaded up his truck and after a running snatch at breakfast was headed back into the mountains. When the news out of Oakland was thrilling around the world he was far into the Sierras.

The summer quarters of Pizzozi were close to Mt. Heckla, whose looming shoulders rose square in the center of the pasture of the three brothers. It was not a noted mountain—that is, until this day—and had no reason for a name other than that it was a peak outstanding from the range; like a thousand others; rugged, pine clad, coated with deer-brush, red soil, and mountain miserie,

It was the deer-brush that gave it value to the Pizzozis—a succulent feed richer than alfalfa. In the early summer they would come up with bony cattle. When they returned in the fall they went out driving beef-steaks. But inland cattle must have more than forage. Salt is the tincture that makes them healthy.

It was far past the time of the regular salting. Pizzozi was in a hurry. It was nine o'clock when he passed through the mining town of Jackson; and by twelve o'clock—the minute of the disaster—he was well beyond the last little hamlet that linked up with civilization. It was four o'clock when he drew up at the little pine-sheltered cabin that was his headquarters for the summer.

He had been on the road since midnight. He was tired. The long weary hours of driving, the grades, the unvaried stress though the deep red dust, the heat, the stretch of a night and day had worn both mind and muscle. It had been his turn to go after salt; now that he was here, he could lie in for a bit of rest while his brothers did the salting.

It was a peaceful spot! this cabin of the Pizzozis; nestled among the virgin shade trees, great tall feathery sugar-pines with a mountain live-oak spreading over the door yard. To the east the rising heights of the Sierras, misty, gray-green, undulating into the distance to the pink-white snow crests of Little Alpine. Below in the canyon, the waters of the Mokolumne; to the west the heavy dark masses of Mt. Heckla, deep verdant in the cool of coming evening.

Joe drew up under the shade of the live oak. The air was full of cool, sweet scent of the afternoon. No moment could have been more peaceful; the blue clear sky overhead, the breath of summer, and the soothing spice of the pine trees. A shepherd dog came bounding from the doorway to meet him.

It was his favorite cow dog. Usually when Joe came back the dog would be far down the road to forestall him. He had wondered, absently, coming up, at the dog's delay. A dog is most of all a creature of habit; only something unusual would detain him. However the dog was here; as the man drew up he rushed out to greet him. A rush, a circle, a bark, and a whine of welcome. Perhaps the dog had been asleep.

But Joe noticed that whine; he was wise in the ways of dogs; when Ponto whined like that there was something unusual. It was not effusive or spontaneous; but rather of the delight of succor. After scarce a minute of patting, the dog squatted and faced to the westward. His whine was startling; almost fearful.

Pizzozi knew that something was wrong. The dog drew up, his stub tail erect, and his hair all bristled; one look was for his master and the other whining and alert to Mt. Heckla. Puzzled, Joe gazed at the mountain. But he saw nothing.

Was it the canine instinct, or was it coincidence? We have the account from Pizzozi. From the words of the Italian, the dog was afraid. It was not the way of Ponto; usually in the face of danger he was alert and eager; now he drew away to the cabin. Joe wondered.

Inside the shack he found nothing but evidence of departure. There was no sign of his brothers. It was his turn to go to sleep; he was wearied almost to numbness, for forty-eight hours he had not closed an eyelid. On the table were a few unwashed dishes and crumbs of eating. One of the three rifles that hung usually on the wall was missing; the coffee pot was on the floor with the lid open. On the bed the coverlets were mussed up. It was a temptation to go to sleep. Back of him the open door and Ponto. The whine of the dog drew his will and his consciousness into correlation. A faint rustle in the sugar-pines soughed from the canyon.

Joe watched the dog. The sun was just glowing over the crest of the mountain; on the western line the deep lacy silhouettes of the pine trees and the bare bald head of Heckla. What was it? His brothers should be on hand for the salting; it was not their custom to put things off for the morrow. Shading his eyes he stepped out of the doorway.

The dog rose stealthily and walked behind him, uneasily, with the same insistent whine and ruffled hair. Joe listened. Only the mountain murmurs, the sweet breath of the forest, and in the lapse of bated breath the rippling melody of the river far below him.

"What you see, Ponto? What you see?"

At the words the dog sniffed and advanced slightly—a growl and then a sudden scurry to the heels of his master. Ponto was afraid. It puzzled Pizzozi. But whatever it was that roused his fear, it was on Mt. Heckla.

This is one of the strange parts of the story—the part the dog played, and what came after. Although it is a trivial thing it is one of the most inexplicable. Did the dog sense it? We have no measure for the range of instinct, but we do have it that before the destruction of Pompeii the beasts roared in their cages. Still, knowing what we now know, it is hard to accept the analogy. It may, after all have been coincidence.

Nevertheless it decided Pizzozi. The cattle needed salt. He would catch up his pinto and ride over to the salt logs.

There is no moment in the cattle industry quite like the salting on the range. It is not the most spectacular perhaps, but surely it is not lacking in intenseness. The way of Pizzozi was musical even if not operatic. He had a long-range call, a rising rhythm that for depth and tone had a peculiar effect on the shattered stillness. It echoed and reverberated, and peeled from the top to the bottom of the mountain. The salt call is the talisman of the mountains.

"Alleewahoo!"

Two thousand cattle augmented by a thousand strays held up their heads in answer. The sniff of the welcome salt call! Through the whole range of the man's voice the stock stopped in their leafy pasture and listened.

"Alleewahoo!"

An old cow bellowed. It was the beginning of bedlam. From the bottom of the mountain to the top and for miles beyond went forth the salt call. Three thousand head bellowed to the delight of salting.

Pizzozi rode along. Each lope of his pinto through the tall tangled miserie was accented. *"Alleewahoo! Alleewahoo!"* The rending of brush, the confusion, and pandemonium spread to the very bottom of the leafy gulches. It is no place for a pedestrian. Heads and tails erect, the cattle were stampeding toward the logs.

A few head had beat him to it. These he quickly drove away and cut the sack open. With haste he poured it upon the logs; then he rode out of the dust that for yards about the place was tramped to the finest powder. The center of a herd of salting range stock is no place for comfort. The man rode away; to the left he ascended a low knob where he would be safe from the stampede; but close enough to distinguish the brands.

In no time the place was alive with milling stock. Old cows, heifers, bulls, calves, steers rushed out of the crashing brush into the clearing. There is no moment exactly like it. What before had been a broad clearing of brownish reddish dust was trampled into a vast cloud of bellowing blur, a thousand cattle, and still coming. From the farthest height came the echoing call. Pizzozi glanced up at the top of the mountain.

And then a strange thing happened.

From what we gathered from the excited accounts of Pizzozi it was instantaneous; and yet by the same words it was of such a peculiar and beautiful effect as never to be forgotten. A bluish azure shot though with a myriad flecks of crimson, a peculiar vividness of opalescence; the whole world scintillating; the sky, the air, the mountain, a vast flame of color so wide and so intense that there seemed not a thing beside it. And instantaneous—it was over almost before it was started. No noise or warning, and no subsequent detonation: as silent as winking and much, indeed, like the queer blur of color induced by defective vision. All in the fraction of a second. Pizzozi had been gazing at the mountain. There was no mountain!

Neither were there cattle. Where before had been the shade of the towering peak was now the rays of the western sun. Where had been the blur of the milling herd and its deafening pandemonium was now a strange silence. The transparency of the air was unbroken into the distance. Far off lay a peaceful range in the sunset. There was no mountain! Neither were there cattle!

For a moment the man had enough to do with his plunging mustang. In the blur of the subsequent second Pizzozi remembers nothing but a convulsion of fighting horseflesh bucking, twisting, plunging, the gentle pinto suddenly maddened into a demon. It required all the skill of the cowman to retain his saddle.

He did not know that he was riding on the rim of Eternity. In his mind was the dim subconscious realization of a thing that had happened. In spite of all his efforts the horse fought backward. It was some moments before he conquered. Then he looked.

It was a slow, hesitant moment. One cannot account for what he will do in the open face of a miracle. What the Italian beheld was enough for terror. The sheer immensity of the thing was too much for thinking.

At the first sight his simplex mind went numb from sheer impotence; his terror to a degree frozen. The whole of Mt.

Heckla had been shorn away; in the place of its darkened shadow the sinking sun was blinking in his face; the whole western sky all golden. There was no vestige of the flat salt-clearing at the base of the mountain. Of the two thousand cattle milling in the dust not a one remained. The man crossed himself in stupor. Mechanically he put the spurs to the pinto.

But the mustang would not. Another struggle with bucking, fighting, maddened horseflesh. The cow-man must needs bring in all the skill of his training; but by the time he had conquered his mind had settled within some scope of comprehension.

The pony had good reasons for his terror. This time though the man's mind reeled it did not go dumb at the clash of immensity. Not only had the whole mountain been torn away, but its roots as well. The whole thing was up-side down; the world torn to its entrails. In place of what had been the height was a gulf so deep that its depths were blackness.

He was standing on the brink. He was a cool man, was Pizzozi; but it was hard in the confusion of such a miracle to think clearly; much less to reason. The prancing mustang was snorting with terror. The man glanced down.

The very dizziness of the gulf, sheer, losing itself into shadows and chaos overpowered him, his mind now clear enough for perception reeled at the distance. The depth was nauseating. His whole body succumbed to a sudden qualm of weakness: the sickness that comes just before falling. He went limp in the saddle.

But the horse fought backward; warned by instinct it drew back from the sheer banks of the gulf. It had no reason but its nature. At the instant it sensed the snapping of the iron will of its master. In a moment it had turned and was racing on its wild way out of the mountains. At supreme moments a cattle horse will always hit for home. The pinto and its limp rider were fleeing on the road to Jackson.

Pizzozi had no knowledge of what had occurred in Oakland. To him the whole thing had been but a flash of miracle; he could not reason. He did not curb his horse. That he was still in the saddle was due more to the near-instinct of his training than to his volition.

He did not even draw up at the cabin. That he could make better time with his motor than with his pinto did not occur to him; his mind was far too busy; and, now that the thing was passed, too full of terror. It was forty-four miles to town; it was night and the stars were shining when he rode into Jackson.

CHAPTER IV
"Man—A Great Little Bug"

AND what of Charley Huyck? It was his anticipation, and his training which leaves us here to tell the story. Were it not for the strange manner of his rearing, and the keen faith and appreciation of Dr. Hobold there would be to-day no tale to tell. The little incident of the burning-glass had grown. If there is no such thing as Fate there is at least something that comes very close to being Destiny.

On this night we find Charley at the observatory in Arizona. He is a grown man and a great one, and though mature not so very far drawn from the lad we met on the street selling papers. Tall, slender, very slightly stooped and with the same idealistic, dreaming eyes of the poet. Surely no one at first glance would have taken him for a scientist. Which he was and was not.

Indeed, there is something vastly different about the

science of Charley Huyck. Science to be sure, but not prosaic. He was the first and perhaps the last of the school of Dr. Robold, a peculiar combination of poetry and fact, a man of vision, of vast, far-seeing faith and idealism linked and based on the coldest and sternest truths of materialism. A peculiar tenet of the theory of Robold: "True science to be itself should be half poetry." Which any of us who have read or been at school know it is not. It is a peculiar theory and though rather wild still with some points in favor.

We all of us know our schoolmasters; especially those of science and what they stand for. Facts, facts, nothing but facts; no dreams or romance. Looking back we can grant them just about the emotions of cucumbers. We remember their cold, hard features, the prodding after fact, the accumulation of data. Surely there is no poetry in them.

Yet we must not deny that they have been by far the most potent of all men in the progress of civilzation[sic]. Not even Robold would deny it.

The point is this:

The doctor maintained that from the beginning the progress of material civilization had been along three distinct channels; science, invention, and administration. It was simply his theory that the first two should be one; that the scientist deal not alone with dry fact but with invention, and that the inventor, unless he is a scientist, has mastered but half his trade. "The really great scientist should be a visionary," said Robold, "and an inventor is merely a poet, with tools."

Which is where we get Charley Huyck. He was a visionary, a scientist, a poet with tools, the protégé of Dr. Robold. He dreamed things that no scientist had thought of. And we are thankful for his dreaming.

The one great friend of Huyck was Professor Williams,

a man from Charley's home city, who had known him even back in the days of selling papers. They had been cronies in boyhood, in their teens, and again at College. In after years, when Huyck had become the visionary, the mysterious Man of the Mountain, and Williams a great professor of astronomy, the friendship was as strong as ever.

But there was a difference between them. Williams was exact to acuteness, with not a whit of vision beyond pure science. He had been reared in the old stone-cold theory of exactness; he lived in figures. He could not understand Huyck or his reasoning. Perfectly willing to follow as far as facts permitted he refused to step off into speculation.

Which was the point between them. Charley Huyck had vision; although exact as any man, he had ever one part of his mind soaring out into speculation. What is, and what might be, and the gulf between. To bridge the gulf was the life work of Charley Huyck.

In the snug little office in Arizona we find them; Charley with his feet poised on the desk and Williams precise and punctilious, true to his training, defending the exactness of his philosophy. It was the cool of the evening; the sun was just mellowing the heat of the desert. Through the open door and windows a cool wind was blowing. Charley was smoking; the same old pipe had been the bane of Williams's life at college.

"Then we know?" he was asking.

"Yes," spoke the professor, "what we know, Charley, we know; though of course it is not much. It is very hard, nay impossible, to deny figures. We have not only the proofs of geology but of astronomical calculation, we have facts and figures plus our sidereal relations all about us.

"The world must come to an end. It is a hard thing to say

it, but it is a fact of science. Slowly, inevitably, ruthlessly, the end will come. A mere question of arithmetic."

Huyck nodded. It was his special function in life to differ with his former roommate. He had come down from his own mountain in Colorado just for the delight of difference.

"I see. Your old calculations of tidal retardation. Or if that doesn't work the loss of oxygen and the water."

"Either one or the other; a matter of figures; the earth is being drawn every day by the sun: its rotation is slowing up; when the time comes it will act to the sun in exactly the same manner as the moon acts to the earth to-day."

"I understand. It will be a case of eternal night for one side of the earth, and eternal day for the other. A case of burn up or freeze up."

"Exactly. Or if it doesn't reach to that, the water gas will gradually lose out into sidereal space and we will go to desert. Merely a question of the old dynamical theory of gases; of the molecules to be in motion, to be forever colliding and shooting out into variance.

"Each minute, each hour, each day we are losing part of our atmospheric envelope. In course of time it will all be gone; when it is we shall be all desert. For intance[sic], take a look outside. This is Arizona. Once it was the bottom of a deep blue sea. Why deny when we can already behold the beginning."

The other laughed.

"Pretty good mathematics at that, professor. Only—"

"Only?"

"That it is merely mathematics."

"Merely mathematics?" The professor frowned slightly. "Mathematics do not lie, Charlie, you cannot get away from them. What sort of fanciful argument are you bringing up now?"

"Simply this," returned the other, "that you depend too much on figures. They are material and in the nature of things can only be employed in a calculation of what *may* happen in the future. You must have premises to stand on, facts. Your figures are rigid: they have no elasticity; unless your foundations are permanent and faultless your deductions will lead you only into error."

"Granted; just the point: we know where we stand. Wherein are we in error?"

It was the old point of difference. Huyck was ever crashing down the idols of pure materialism. Williams was of the world-wide school.

"You are in error, my dear professor, in a very little thing and a very large one."

"What is that?"

"Man."

"Man?"

"Yes. He's a great little bug. You have left him out of your calculation—which he will upset."

The professor smiled indulgently. "I'll allow; he is at least a conceited bug; but you surely cannot grant him much when pitted against the Universe."

"No? Did it ever occur to you, Professor, what the Universe is? The stars for instance? Space, the immeasurable distance of Infinity. Have you never dreamed?"

Williams could not quite grasp him. Huyck had a habit that had grown out of childhood. Always he would allow his opponent to commit himself. The professor did not answer. But the other spoke.

"Ether. You know it. Whether mind or granite. For instance, your desert." He placed his finger to his forehead. "Your mind, my mind—localized ether."

"What are you driving at?"

"Merely this. Your universe has intelligence. It has mind as well as matter. The little knot called the earth is becoming conscious. Your deductions are incompetent unless they embrace mind as well as matter, and they cannot do it. Your mathematics are worthless."

The professor bit his lip.

"Always fanciful.." he commented, "and visionary. Your argument is beautiful, Charley, and hopeful. I would that it were true. But all things must mature. Even an earth must die."

"Not our earth. You look into the past, professor, for your proof, and I look into the future. Give a planet long enough time in maturing and it will develop life; give it still longer and it will produce intelligence. Our own earth is just coming into consciousness; it has thirty million years, at least, to run."

"You mean?"

"This. That man is a great little bug. Mind: the intelligence of the earth."

This of course is a bit dry. The conversation of such men very often is to those who do not care to follow them. But it is very pertinent to what came after. We know now, everyone knows, that Charley Huyck was right. Even Professor Williams admits it. Our earth is conscious. In less than twenty-four hours it had to employ its consciousness to save itself from destruction.

A bell rang. It was the private wire that connected the office with the residence. The professor picked up the receiver. "Just a minute. Yes? All right." Then to his companion: "I must go over to the house, Charley. We have plenty of time. Then we can go up to the observatory."

Which shows how little we know about ourselves. Poor

Professor Williams! Little did he think that those casual words were the last he would ever speak to Charley Huyck.

The whole world seething! The beginning of the end! Charley Huyck in the vortex. The next few hours were to be the most strenuous of the planet's history.

CHAPTER V
Approaching Disaster

IT was night. The stars which had just been coming out were spotted by millions over the sleeping desert. One of the nights that are peculiar to the country, which we all of us know so well, if not from experience, at least from hearsay; mellow, soft, sprinkled like salted fire, twinkling.

Each little light a message out of infinity. Cosmic grandeur; mind: chaos, eternity—a night for dreaming. Whoever had chosen the spot in the desert had picked full well. Charley had spoken of consciousness. On that night when he gazed up at the stars he was its personification. Surely a good spirit was watching over the earth.

A cool wind was blowing; on its breath floated the murmurs from the village; laughter, the song of children, the purring of motors and the startled barking of a dog; the confused drone of man and his civilization. From the eminence the observatory looked down upon the town and the sheen of light, spotting like jewels in the dim glow of the desert. To the east the mellow moon just tipping over the mountain. Charley stepped to the window.

He could see it all. The subtle beauty that was so akin to poetry: the stretch of desert, the mountains, the light in the eastern sky; the dull level shadow that marked the plain to the northward. To the west the mountains looming black to the star line. A beautiful night; sweetened with the breath of desert and tuned to its slumber.

Across the lawn he watched the professor descending the pathway under the acacias. An automobile was coming up the driveway; as it drove up under the arcs he noticed its powerful lines and its driver; one of those splendid pleasure cars that have returned to favor during the last decade; the soft purr of its motor, the great heavy tires and its coating of dust. There is a lure about a great car coming in from the desert. The car stopped, Charley noted. Doubtless some one for Williams. If it were, he would go into the observatory alone.

In the strict sense of the word Huyck was not an astronomer. He had not made it his profession. But for all that he knew things about the stars that the more exact professors had not dreamed of. Charley was a dreamer. He had a code all his own and a manner of reasoning. Between him and the stars lay a secret.

He had not divulged it, or if he had, it was in such an open way that it was laughed at. It was not cold enough in calculation or, even if so, was too far from their deduction. Huyck had imagination; his universe was alive and potent; it had intelligence. Matter could not live without it. Man was its manifestation; just come to consciousness. The universe teemed with intelligence. Charley looked at the stars.

He crossed the office, passed through the reception-room and thence to the stairs that led to the observatory. In the time that would lapse before the coming of his friend he would have ample time for observation. Somehow he felt that there was time for discovery. He had come down to Arizona to employ the lens of his friend the astronomer. The instrument that he had erected on his own mountain in Colorado had not given him the full satisfaction that he expected. Here in

Arizona, in the dry clear air, which had hitherto given such splendid results, he hoped to find what he was after. But little did he expect to discover the terrible thing he did.

It is one of the strangest parts of the story that he should be here at the very moment when Fate and the world's safety would have had him. For years he and Dr. Robold had been at work on their visionary projects. They were both dreamers. While others had scoffed they had silently been at their great work on kinetics.

The boy and the burning glass had grown under the tutelage of Dr. Robold: the time was about at hand when he could out-rival the saying of Archimedes. Though the world knew it not, Charley Huyck had arrived at the point where he could literally burn up the earth.

But he was not sinister; though he had the power he had of course not the slightest intention. He was a dreamer and it was part of his dream that man break his thraldom to the earth and reach out into the universe. It was a great conception and were it not for the terrible event which took his life we have no doubt but that he would have succeeded.

It was ten-thirty when he mounted the steps and seated himself. He glanced at his watch: he had a good ten minutes. He had computed before just the time for the observation. For months he had waited for just this moment; he had not hoped to be alone and now that he was in solitary possession he counted himself fortunate. Only the stars and Charley Huyck knew the secret; and not even he dreamed what it would amount to.

From his pocket he drew a number of papers; most of them covered with notations; some with drawings; and a good sized map in colors. This he spread before him, and with his pencil began to draw right across its face a net of lines and cross lines. A number of figures and a rapid computation. He nodded and then he made the observation.

It would have been interesting to study the face of Charley Huyck during the next few moments. At first he was merely receptive, his face placid but with the studious intentness of one who has come to the moment: and as he began to find what he was after—an eagerness of satisfaction. Then a queer blankness; the slight movement of his body stopped, and the tapping of his feet ceased entirely.

For a full five minutes an absolute intentness. During that time he was out among the stars beholding what not even he had dreamed of. It was more than a secret: and what it was only Charley Huyck of all the millions of men could have recognized. Yet it was more than even he had expected. When he at last drew away his face was chalk-like; great drops of sweat stood on his forehead: and the terrible truth in his eyes made him look ten years older.

"My God!"

For a moment indecision and strange impotence. The truth he had beheld numbed action; from his lips the mumbled words:

"This world; my world; our great and splendid mankind!"

A sentence that was despair and a benediction.

Then mechanically he turned back to confirm his observation. This time, knowing what he would see, he was not so horrified: his mind was cleared by the plain fact of what he was beholding. When at last he drew away his face was settled.

He was a man who thought quickly—thank the stars for that—and, once he thought, quick to spring to action. There was a peril poising over the earth. If it were to be voided there was not a second to lose in weighing up the possibilities.

He had been dreaming all his life. He had never thought that the climax was to be the very opposite of what he hoped for. In his under mind he prayed for Dr. Robold—dead and gone forever. Were he only here to help him!

He seized a piece of paper. Over its white face he ran a mass of computations. He worked like lightning; his fingers plying and his mind keyed to the pin-point of genius. Not one thing did he overlook in his calculation. If the earth had a chance he would find it.

There are always possibilities. He was working out the odds of the greatest race since creation. While the whole world slept, while the uncounted millions lay down in fond security, Charley Huyck there in the lonely room on the desert drew out their figured odds to the point of infinity.

"Just one chance in a million."

He was going to take it. The words were not out of his mouth before his long legs were leaping down the stairway. In the flash of seconds his mind was rushing into clear action. He had had years of dreaming; all his years of study and tutelage under Robold gave him just the training for such a disaster.

But he needed time. Time! Time! Why was it so precious? He must get to his own mountain. In six jumps he was in the office.

It was empty. The professor had not returned. He thought rather grimly and fleetingly of their conversation a few minutes before; what would Williams think now of science and consciousness? He picked up the telephone receiver. While he waited he saw out of the corner of his eye the car in the driveway. It was—

"Hello. The professor? What? Gone down to town? No! Well, say, this is Charley"—he was watching the car in front of the building, "Say, hello—tell him I have gone home, home!

H-o-m-e to Colorado—to Colorado, yes—to the mountain—the m-o-u-n-t-a-i-n. Oh, never mind—I'll leave a note.

He clamped down the receiver. On the desk he scrawled on a piece of paper:

> ED:
>
> "Look these up. I'm bound for the mountain. No time to explain. There's a car outside. Stay with the lens. Don't leave it. If the earth goes up you will know that I have not reached the mountain."

Beside the note he placed one of the maps that he had in his pocket—with his pencil drew a black cross just above the center. Under the map were a number of computations.

It is interesting to note that in the stress of the great critical moment he forgot the professor's title. It was a good thing. When Williams read it he recognized the significance. All through their life in crucial moments he had been "Ed." to Charley.

But the note was all he was destined to find. A brisk wind was blowing. By a strange balance of fate the same movement that let Huyck out of the building ushered in the wind and upset calculation.

It was a little thing, but it was enough to keep all the world in ignorance and despair. The eddy whisking in through the door picked up the precious map, poised it like a tiny plane, and dropped it neatly behind a bookcase.

CHAPTER VI
A Race to Save the World

HUYCK was working in a straight line. Almost before his last words on the phone were spoken he had requisitioned that automobile outside; whether money or talk, faith or force, he was going to have it. The hum of the motor sounded in his ears as he ran down the steps. He was hatless and in his shirt-sleeves. The driver was just putting some tools in the car. With one jump Charley had him by the collar.

"Five thousand dollars if you can get me to Robold Mountain in twenty hours."

The very suddenness of the rush caught the man by surprise and lurched him against the car, turning him half around. Charley found himself gazing into dull brown eyes and sardonic laughter: a long, thin nose and lips drooped at the corners, then as suddenly tipping up—a queer creature, half devil, half laughter, and all fun.

"Easy, Charley, easy! How much did you say? Whisper it."

It was Bob Winters. Bob Winters and his car. And waiting. Surely no twist of fortune could nave been greater. He was a college chum of Huyck's and of the professor's. If there was one man that could make the run in the time allotted, Bob was he. But Huyck was impersonal. With the burden on his mind he thought of naught but his destination.

"Ten thousand!" he shouted.

The man held back his head. Huyck was far too serious to appreciate mischief. But not the man.

"Charley Huyck, of all men. Did young Lochinvar come out of the West? How much did you say? This desert air and the dust, 'tis hard on the hearing. She must be a young, fair maiden. Ten thousand."

"Twenty thousand. Thirty thousand. Damnation, man, you can have the mountain. Into the car."

By sheer subjective strength he forced the other into the machine. It was not until they were shooting out of the grounds on two wheels that he realized that the man was

Bob Winters. Still the workings of fate.

The madcap and wild Bob of the races! Surely Destiny was on the job. The challenge of speed and the premium. At the opportune moment before disaster the two men were brought together. Minutes weighed up with centuries and hours out-balanced millenniums. The whole world slept; little did it dream that its very life was riding north with these two men into the midnight.

Into the midnight! The great car, the pride of Winter's heart, leaped between the pillars. At the very outset, madcap that he was, he sent her into seventy miles an hour; they fairly jumped off the hill into the village. At a full seventy-five he took the curve; she skidded, sheered half around and swept on.

For an instant Charley held his breath. But the master hand held her; she steadied, straightened, and shot out into the desert. Above the whir of the motor, flying dust and blurring what-not, Charley got the tones of his companion's voice. He had heard the words somewhere in history.

"Keep your seat, Mr. Greely. Keep your seat!"

The moon was now far up over the mountain, the whole desert was bathed in a mellow twilight; in the distance the mountains brooded like an uncertain slumbering cloud bank. They were headed straight to the northward; though there was a better road round about, Winters had chosen the hard, rocky bee-line to the mountain.

He knew Huyck and his reputation; when Charley offered thirty thousand for a twenty-hour drive it was not mere byplay. He had happened in at the observatory to drop in on Williams on his way to the coast. They had been classmates; likewise he and Charley.

When the excited man out of the observatory had seized him by the collar, Winters merely had laughed. He was the speed king. The three boys who had gone to school were now playing with the destiny of the earth. But only Huyck knew it.

Winters wondered. Through miles and miles of fleeting sagebrush, cacti and sand and desolation, he rolled over the problem. Steady as a rock, slightly stooped, grim and as certain as steel he held to the north. Charley Huyck by his side, hatless, coatless, his hair dancing to the wind, all impatience. Why was it? Surely a man even for death would have time to get his hat.

The whole thing spelled speed to Bob Winters; perhaps it was the infusion of spirit or the intensity of his companion; but the thrill ran into his vitals. Thirty thousand dollars—for a stake like that—what was the balance? He had been called Wild Bob for his daring; some had called him insane; on this night his insanity was enchantment.

It was wild; the lee of the giant roadster a whirring shower of gravel: into the darkness, into the night the car fought over the distance. The terrific momentum and the friction of the air fought in their faces; Huyck's face was unprotected: in no time his lips were cracked, and long before they had crossed the level his whole face was bleeding.

But he heeded it not. He only knew that they were moving; that slowly, minute by minute, they were cutting down the odds that bore disaster. In his mind a maze of figures; the terrible sight he had seen in the telescope and the thing impending. Why had he kept his secret?

Over and again he impeached himself and Dr. Robold. It had come to this. The whole world sleeping and only himself to save it. Oh, for a few minutes, for one short moment! Would he get it?

At last they reached the mountains. A rough, rocky road, and but little traveled. Happily Winters had made it once before, and knew it. He took it with every bit of speed they could stand, but even at that it was diminished to a minimum.

For hours they fought over grades and gulches, dry washouts and boulders. It was dawn, and the sky was growing pink when they rode down again upon the level. It was here that they ran across their first trouble; and it was here that Winters began to realize vaguely what a race they might be running.

The particular level which they had entered was an elbow of the desert projecting into the mountains just below a massive, newly constructed dam. The reservoir had but lately been filled, and all was being put in readiness for the dedication.

An immense sheet of water extending far back into the mountains—it was intended before long to transform the desert into a garden. Below, in the valley, was a town, already the center of a prosperous irrigation settlement; but soon, with the added area, to become a flourishing city. The elbow, where they struck it, was perhaps twenty miles across. Their northward path would take them just outside the tip where the foothills of the opposite mountain chain melted into the desert. Without ado Winters put on all speed and plunged across the sands. And then:

It was much like winking; but for all that something far more impressive. To Winters, on the left hand of the car and with the east on the right hand, it was much as if the sun had suddenly leaped up and as suddenly plumped down behind the horizon—a vast vividness of scintillating opalescence: an azure, naming diamond shot by a million fire points.

Instantaneous and beautiful. In the pale dawn of the desert air its wonder and color were beyond all beauty. Winters caught it out of the corner of his eye; it was so instantaneous and so illusive that he was not certain. Instinctively he looked to his companion.

But Charley, too, had seen it. His attitude of waiting and hoping was vigorized into vivid action. He knew just what it was. With one hand he clutched Winters and fairly shouted.

"On, on, Bob! On, as you value your life. Put into her every bit of speed you have got."

At the same instant, at the same breath came a roar that was not to be forgotten; crunching, rolling, terrible—like the mountain moving.

Bob knew it. It was the dam. Something had broken it. To the east the great wall of water fallout of the mountains! A beautiful sight and terrible; a relentless glassy roller fringed along its base by a lace of racing foam. The upper part was as smooth as crystal; the stored-up waters of the mountain moving out compactly. The man thought of the little town below and its peril. But Huyck thought also. He shouted in Winter's ear:

"Never mind the town. Keep straight north. Over yonder to the point of the water. The town will have to drown."

It was inexorable; there was no pity; the very strength and purpose of the command drove into the other's understanding. Dimly now he realized that they were really running a race against time. Winters was a daredevil; the very catastrophe sent a thrill of exultation through him. It was the climax, the great moment of his life, to be driving at a hundred miles an hour under that wall of water.

The roar was terrible, Before they were half across it seemed to the two men that the very sound would drown them. There was nothing in the world but pandemonium. The strange flash was forgotten in the terror of the living wall that was reaching out to engulf them. Like insects they whizzed in the open face of the deluge. When they had reached the tip they were so close that the outrunning fringe of the surf was at their wheels.

Around the point with the wide open plain before them. With the flood behind them it was nothing to outrun it. The waters with a wider stretch spread out. In a few moments they had left all behind them.

But Winters wondered; what was the strange flash of evanescent beauty? He knew this dam and its construction; to outlast the centuries. It had been whiffed in a second. It was not lightning. He had heard no sound other than the rush of the waters. He looked to his companion.

Hueyk nodded.

"That's the thing we are racing. We have only a few hours. Can we make it?"

Bob had thought that he was getting all the speed possible out of his motor. What it yielded from that moment on was a revelation.

It is not safe and hardly possible to be driving at such speed on the desert. Only the best car and a firm roadway can stand it. A sudden rut, squirrel hole, or pocket of sand is as good as destruction. They rushed on till noon.

Not even Winters, with all his alertness, could avoid it. Perhaps he was weary. The tedious hours, the racking speed had worn him to exhaustion. They had ceased to individualize, their way a blur, a nightmare of speed and distance.

It came suddenly, a blind barranca—one of those sunken, useless channels that are death to the unwary. No warning.

It was over just that quickly. A mere flash of consciousness plus a sensation of flying. Two men broken on the sands and the great, beautiful roadster a twisted ruin.

CHAPTER VII
A Riven Continent

BUT back to the world. No one knew about Charley Huyck nor what was occurring on the desert. Even if we had it would have been impossible to construe connection.

After the news out of Oakland, and the destruction of Mt. Heckla, we were far too appalled. The whole thing was beyond us. Not even the scientists with all their data could find one thing to work on. The wires of the world buzzed with wonder and with panic. We were civilized. It is really strange how quickly, in spite of our boasted powers, we revert to the primitive.

Superstition cannot die. Where was no explanation must be miracle. The thing had been repeated. When would it strike again. And where?

There was not long to wait. But this time the stroke was of far more consequence and of far more terror. The sheer might of the thing shook the earth. Not a man or government that would not resign in the face of such destruction.

It was omnipotent. A whole continent had been riven. It would be impossible to give description of such catastrophe; no pen can tell it any more than it could describe the creation. We can only follow in its path.

On the morning after the first catastrophe, at eight o'clock, just south of the little city of Santa Cruz, on the north shore of the Bay of Monterey, the same light and the same, though not quite the same, instantaneousness. Those who beheld it report a vast ball of azure blue and opalescent fire and motion; a strange sensation of vitalized vibration; of personified living force. In shape like a marble, as round as a full moon in its glory, but of infinitely more beauty.

It came from nowhere; neither from above the earth nor below it. Seeming to leap out of nothing, it glided or rather vanished to the eastward. Still the effect of winking, though this time, perhaps from a distanced focus, more vivid. A dot or marble, like a full moon, burning, opal, soaring to the eastward.

And instantaneous. Gone as soon as it was come; noiseless and of phantom beauty; like a finger of the Omnipotent tracing across the world, and as terrible. The human mind had never conceived a thing so vast.

Beginning at the sands of the ocean the whole country had vanished; a chasm twelve miles wide and of unknown depth running straight to the eastward. Where had been farms and homes was nothing; the mountains had been seared like butter. Straight as an arrow.

Then the roar of the deluge. The waters of the Pacific breaking through its sands and rolling into the Gulf of Mexico. That there was no heat was evidenced by the fact that there was no steam. The thing could not be internal. Yet what was it?

One can only conceive in figures. From the shores of Santa Cruz to the Atlantic—a few seconds; then out into the eastern ocean straight out into the Sea of the Sargasso. A great gulf riven straight across the face of North America.

The path seemed to follow the sun; it bore to the eastward with a slight southern deviation. The mountains it cut like cheese. Passing just north of Fresno it seared through the gigantic Sierras halfway between the Yosemite and Mt. Whitney, through the great desert to southern Nevada, thence across northern Arizona, New Mexico, Texas, Arkansas, Mississippi, Alabama, and Georgia, entering the Atlantic at a point half-way between Brunswick and Jacksonville. A great canal twelve miles in width linking the oceans. A cataclysmic blessing. Today, with thousands of ships bearing freight over its water, we can bless that part of the disaster.

But there was more to come. So far the miracle had been sporadic. Whatever had been its force it had been fatal only on point and occasion. In a way it had been local. The deadly atmospheric combination of its aftermath was invariable in its recession. There was no suffering. The death that it dealt was the death of obliteration. But now it entered on another stage.

The world is one vast ball, and, though large, still a very small place to live in. There are few of us, perhaps, who look upon it, or even stop to think of it, as a living being. Yet it is just that. It has its currents, life, pulse, and its fevers; it is coordinate; a million things such as the great streams of the ocean, the swirls of the atmosphere, make it a place to live in. And we are conscious only, or mostly, through disaster.

A strange thing happened.

The great opal like a mountain of fire had riven across the continent. From the beginning and with each succession the thing was magnified. But it was not until it had struck the waters of the Atlantic that we became aware of its full potency and its fatality.

The earth quivered at the shock, and man stood on his toes in terror. In twenty-four hours our civilization was literally falling to pieces. We were powerful with the forces that we understood; but against this that had been literally ripped from the unknown we were insignificant. The whole world was frozen. Let us see.

Into the Atlantic! The transition. Hitherto silence. But now the roar of ten thousand million Niagaras, the waters of the ocean rolling, catapulting, roaring into the gulf that had been seared in its bosom. The Gulf Stream cut in two, the currents that tempered our civilization sheared in a second. Straight into the Sargasso Sea. The great opal, liquid fire, luminiscent, a ball like the setting sun, lay poised upon the ocean. It was the end of the earth!

What was this thing? The whole world knew of it in a second. And not a one could tell. In less than forty hours after its first appearance in Oakland it had consumed a mountain, riven a continent, and was drinking up an ocean. The tangled sea of the Sargasso, dead calm for ages, was a cataract; a swirling torrent of maddened waters rushed to the opal—and disappeared.

It was hellish and out of madness; as beautiful as it was uncanny. The opal high as the Himalayas brooding upon the water; its myriad colors blending, winking in a phantasm of iridescence. The beauty of its light could be seen a thousand miles. A thing out of mystery and out of forces. We had discovered many things and knew much; but had guessed no such thing as this. It was vampirish, and it was literally drinking up the earth.

Consequences were immediate. The point of contact was fifty miles across, the waters of the Atlantic with one accord turned to the magnet. The Gulf Stream veered straight from its course and out across the Atlantic. The icy currents from the poles freed from the warmer barrier descended along the coasts and thence out into the Sargasso Sea. The temperature of the temperate zone dipped below the point of a blizzard.

The first word come out of London. Freezing! And in July! The fruit and entire harvest of northern Europe destroyed. Olympic games at Copenhagen postponed by a foot of snow. The river Seine frozen. Snow falling in New York. Crops nipped with frost as far south as Cape Hatteras.

A fleet of airplanes was despatched from the United States

and another from the west coast of Africa. Not half of them returned. Those that did reported even more disaster. The reports that were handed in were appalling. They had sailed straight on. It was like flying into the sun; the vividness of the opalescence was blinding, rising for miles above them alluring, drawing and unholy, and of a beauty that was terror.

Only the tardy had escaped. It even drew their motors, it was like gravity suddenly become vitalized and conscious. Thousands of machines vaulted into the opalescence. From those ahead hopelessly drawn and powerless came back the warning. But hundreds could not escape.

"Back," came the wireless. "Do not come too close. The thing is a magnet. Turn back before too late. Against this man is insignificant."

Then like gnats flitting into fire they vanished into the opalescence.

The others turned back. The whole world freezing shuddered in horror. A great vampire was brooding over the earth. The greatness that man had attained to was nothing. Civilization was tottering in a day. We were hopeless.

Then came the last revelation; the truth and verity of the disaster and the threatened climax. The water level of all the coast had gone down. Vast ebb tides had gone out not to return. Stretches of sand where had been surf extended far out into the sea. Then the truth! The thing, whatever it was, was drinking up the ocean.

CHAPTER VIII
The Man Who Saved the Earth

IT was tragic; grim, terrible, cosmic. Out of nowhere had come this thing that was eating up the earth. Not a thing out of all our science had there been to warn us;

not a word from all our wise men. We who had built up our civilization, piece by piece, were after all but insects.

We were going out in a maze of beauty into the infinity whence we came. Hour by hour the great orb of opalescence grew in splendor; the effect and the beauty of its lure spread about the earth; thrilling, vibrant like suppressed music. The old earth helpless. Was it possible that out of her bosom she could not pluck one intelligence to save her? Was there not one law—no answer?

Out on the desert with his face to the sun lay the answer. Though almost hopeless there was still some time and enough of near-miracle to save us. A limping fate in the shape of two Indians and a battered runabout at the last moment.

Little did the two red men know the value of the two men found that day on the desert. To them the debris of the mighty car and the prone bodies told enough of the story. They were Samaritans; but there are many ages to bless them.

As it was there were many hours lost. Without this loss there would have been thousands spared and an almost immeasurable amount of disaster. But we have still to be thankful. Charley Huyck was still living.

He had been stunned; battered, bruised, and unconscious; but he had not been injured vitally. There was still enough left of him to drag himself to the old runabout and call for Winters. His companion, as it happened, was in even better shape than himself, and waiting. We do not know how they talked the red men out of their relic—whether by coaxing, by threat, or by force.

Straight north. Two men battered, worn, bruised, but steadfast, bearing in that limping old motor-car the destiny of the earth. Fate was still on the job, but badly crippled.

They had lost many precious hours. Winters had forfeited

his right to the thirty thousand. He did not care. He understood vaguely that there was a stake over and above all money. Huyck said nothing; he was too maimed and too much below will-power to think of speaking. What had occurred during the many hours of their unconsciousness was unknown to them. It was not until they came sheer upon the gulf that had been riven straight across the continent that the awful truth dawned on them.

To Winters it was terrible. The mere glimpse of that blackened chasm was terror. It was bottomless; so deep that its depths were cloudy; the misty haze of its uncertain shadows was akin to chaos. He understood vaguely that it was related to that terrible thing they had beheld in the morning. It was not the power of man. Some force had been loosened which was ripping the earth to its vitals. Across the terror of the chasm he made out the dim outlines of the opposite wall. A full twelve miles across.

For a moment the sight overcame even Huyck himself. Full well he knew; but knowing, as he did, the full fact of the miracle was even more than he expected. His long years under Robold, his scientific imagination had given him comprehension. Not puny steam, nor weird electricity, but force, kinetics—out of the universe.

He knew. But knowing as he did, he was overcome by the horror. Such a thing turned loose upon the earth! He had lost many hours; he had but a few hours remaining. The thought gave him sudden energy. He seized Winters by the arm.

"To the first town, Bob. To the first town—an aerodome."

There was speed in that motor for all its decades. Winters turned about and shot out in a lateral course parallel to the great chasm. But for all his speed he could not keep back his question.

"In the name of Heaven, Charley, what did it? What is it?"

Came the answer; and it drove the lust of all speed through Winters:

"Bob," said Charley, "it is the end of the world—if we don't make it. But a few hours left. We must have an airplane. I must make the mountain."

It was enough for Wild Bob. He settled down. It was only an old runabout; but he could get speed out of a wheelbarrow. He had never driven a race like this. Just once did he speak. The words were characteristic.

"A world's record, Charley. And we're going to win. Just watch us."

And they did.

There was no time lost in the change. The mere fact of Huyck's name, his appearance and the manner of his arrival was enough. For the last hours messages had been pouring in at every post in the Rocky Mountains for Charley Huyck. After the failure of all others many thousands had thought of him.

Even the government, unappreciative before, had awakened to a belated and almost frantic eagerness. Orders were out that everything, no matter what, was to be at his disposal. He had been regarded as visionary; but in the face of what had occurred, visions were now the most practical things for mankind. Besides, Professor Williams had sent out to the world the strange portent of Huyck's note. For years there had been mystery on that mountain. Could it be?

Unfortunately we cannot give it the description we would like to give. Few men outside of the regular employees have ever been to the Mountain of Robold. From the very first, owing perhaps to the great forces stored, and the danger of carelessness, strangers and visitors had been barred. Then, too, the secrecy of Dr. Robold—and the respect of his successor. But we do know that the burning glass had grown into the mountain.

Bob Winters and the aviator are the only ones to tell us; the employees, one and all, chose to remain. The cataclysm that followed destroyed the work of Huyck and Robold—but not until it had served the greatest deed that ever came out of the minds of men. And had it not been for Huyck's insistence we would not have even the account that we are giving.

It was he who insisted, nay, begged, that his companions return while there was yet a chance. Full well he knew. Out of the universe, out of space he had coaxed the forces that would burn up the earth. The great ball of luminous opalescence, and the diminishing ocean!

There was but one answer. Through the imaginative genius of Robold and Huyck, fate had worked up to the moment. The lad and the burning glass had grown to Archimedes.

What happened?

The plane neared the Mountain of Robold. The great bald summit and the four enormous globes of crystal. At least we so assume. We have Winter's word and that of the aviator that they were of the appearance of glass. Perhaps they were not; but we can assume it for description. So enormous that were they set upon a plain they would have overtopped the highest building ever constructed; though on the height of the mountain, and in its contrast, they were not much more than golf balls.

It was not their size but their effect that was startling. They were alive. At least that is what we have from Winters. Living, luminous, burning, twisting within with a thousand blending, iridescent beautiful colors. Not like electricity but something infinitely more powerful. Great mysterious magnets that

Huyck had charged out of chaos. Glowing with the softest light; the whole mountain brightened as in a dream, and the town of Robold at its base lit up with a beauty that was past beholding.

It was new to Winters. The great buildings and the enormous machinery. Engines of strangest pattern, driven by forces that the rest of the world had not thought of. Not a sound; the whole works a complicated mass covering a hundred acres, driving with a silence that was magic. Not a whir nor friction. Like a living composite body pulsing and breathing the strange and mysterious force that had been evolved from Huyck's theory of kinetics. The four great steel conduits running from the globes down the side of the mountain. In the center, at a point midway between the globes, a massive steel needle hung on a pivot and pointed directly at the sun.

Winters and the aviator noted it and wondered. From the lower end of the needle was pouring a luminous stream of pale-blue opalescence, a stream much like a liquid, and of an unholy, radiance. But it was not a liquid, nor fire, nor anything seen by man before.

It was force. We have no better description than the apt phrase of Winters. Charley Huyck was milking the sun, as it dropped from the end of the four living streams to the four globes that took it into storage. The four great, wonderful living globes; the four batteries; the very sight of their imprisoned beauty and power was magnetic.

The genius of Huyck and Robold! Nobody but the wildest dreamers would have conceived it. The life of the sun. And captive to man; at his will and volition. And in the next few minutes we were to lose it all! But in losing it we were to save ourselves. It was fate and nothing else.

There was but one thing more upon the mountain—the observatory and another needle apparently idle; but with a point much like a gigantic phonograph needle. It rose square out of the observatory, and to Winters it gave an impression of a strange gun, or some implement for sighting.

That was all. Coming with the speed that they were making, the airmen had no time for further investigation. But even this is comprehensive. Minus the force. If we only knew more about that or even its theory we might perhaps reconstruct the work of Charley Huyck and Dr. Robold.

They made the landing. Winters, with his nature, would be in at the finish; but Charley would not have it.

"It is death, Bob," he said. "You have a wife and babies. Go back to the world. Go back with all the speed you can get out of your motors. Get as far away as you can before the end comes."

With that he bade them a sad farewell. It was the last spoken word that the outside world had from Charley Huyck.

The last seen of him he was running up the steps of his office. As they soared away and looked back they could see men, the employees, scurrying about in frantic haste to their respective posts and stations. What was it all about? Little did the two aviators know. Little did they dream that it was the deciding stroke.

CHAPTER IX
The Most Terrific Moment in History

STILL the great ball of Opalescence brooding over the Sargasso. Europe now was frozen, and though it was midsummer had gone into winter quarters. The Straits of Dover were no more. The waters had receded and one could walk, if careful, dry-shod from the shores of France to the chalk cliffs of England. The Straits of Gibraltar had dried up. The Mediterranean completely land-locked, was cut off forever from the tides of the mother ocean.

The whole world going dry; not in ethics, but in reality. The great Vampire, luminous, beautiful beyond all ken and thinking, drinking up our life-blood. The Atlantic a vast whirlpool.

A strange frenzy had fallen over mankind: men fought in the streets and died in madness. It was fear of the Great Unknown, and hysteria. At such a moment the veil of civilization was torn to tatters. Man was reverting to the primeval.

Then came the word from Charley Huyck; flashing and repeating to every clime and nation. In its assurance it was almost as miraculous as the Vampire itself. For man had surrendered.

> TO THE PEOPLE OF THE WORLD:
>
> The strange and terrible Opalescence which, for the past seventy hours, has been playing havoc with the world, is not miracle, nor of the supernatural, but a mere manifestation and result of the application of celestial kinetics. Such a thing always was and always will be possible where there is intelligence to control and harness the forces that lie about us. Space is not space exactly, but an infinite cistern of unknown laws and forces. We may control certain laws on earth, but until we reach out farther we are but playthings.
>
> Man is the intelligence of the earth. The time will come when he must be the intelligence of a great deal of space as well. At the present time you are merely fortunate and a victim of a kind fate. That I am the instrument of the earth's salvation is merely chance. The real man is Dr. Robold.

When he picked me up on the streets I had no idea that the sequence of time would drift to this moment. He took me into his work and taught me.

Because he was sensitive and was laughed at, we worked in secret. And since his death, and out of respect to his memory, I have continued in the same manner. But I have written down everything, all the laws, computations, formulas—everything; and I am now willing it to mankind.

Robold had a theory on kinetics. It was strange at first and a thing to laugh at; but he reduced it to laws as potent and as inexorable as the laws of gravitation.

The luminous Opalescence that has almost destroyed us is but one of its minor manifestations. It is a message of sinister intelligence; for back of it all is an Intelligence. Yet it is not all sinister. It is self-preservation. The time is coming when eons of ages from now our own man will be forced to employ just such a weapon for his own preservation. Either that or we shall die of thirst and agony.

Let me ask you to remember now, that whatever you have suffered, you have saved a world. I shall now save you and the earth.

In the vaults you will find everything. All the knowledge and discoveries of the great Dr. Robold, plus a few minor findings by myself.

And now I bid you farewell. You shall soon be free.

CHARLEY HUYCK.

A strange message. Spoken over the wireless and flashed to every clime, it roused and revived the hope of mankind. Who was this Charley Huyck? Uncounted millions of men had never heard his name; there were but few, very few who had.

A message out of nowhere and of very dubious and

doubtful explanation. Celestial kinetics! Undoubtedly. But the words explained nothing. However, man was ready to accept anything, so long as it saved him.

For a more lucid explanation we must go back to the Arizona observatory and Professor Ed. Williams. And a strange one it was truly; a certain proof that consciousness is more potent, far more so than mere material; also that many laws of our astronomers are very apt to be overturned in spite of their mathematics.

Charley Huyck was right. You cannot measure intelligence with a yard-stick. Mathematics do not lie; but when applied to consciousness they are very likely to kick backward. That is precisely what had happened.

The suddenness of Huyck's departure had puzzled Professor Williams; that, and the note which he found upon the table. It was not like Charley to go off so in the stress of a moment. He had not even taken the time to get his hat and coat. Surely something was amiss.

He read the note carefully, and with a deal of wonder.

"Look these up. Keep by the lens. If the world goes up you will know I have not reached the mountain."

What did he mean? Besides, there was no data for him to work on. He did not know that an errant breeze, had plumped the information behind the bookcase. Nevertheless he went into the observatory, and for the balance of the night stuck by the lens.

Now there are uncounted millions of stars in the sky. Williams had nothing to go by. A needle in the hay-stack were an easy task compared with the one that he was allotted. The flaming mystery, whatever it was that Huyck had seen, was not caught by the professor. Still, he wondered. "If the world goes up you will know I have not reached the mountain."

What was the meaning?

But he was not worried. The professor loved Huyck as a visionary and smiled not a little at his delightful fancies. Doubtless this was one of them. It was not until the news came flashing out of Oakland that he began to take it seriously. Then followed the disappearance of Mount Heckla. "If the world goes up"—it began to look as if the words had meaning.

There was a frantic professor during the next few days. When he was not with the lens he was flashing out messages to the world for Charley Huyck. He did not know that Huyck was lying unconscious and almost dead upon the desert. That the world was coming to catastrophe he knew full well; but where was the man to save it? And most of all, what had his friend meant by the words, "look these up"?

Surely there must be some further information. Through the long, long hours he stayed with the lens and waited. And he found nothing.

It was three days. Who will ever forget them? Surely not Professor Williams. He was sweating blood. The whole world was going to pieces without the trace of an explanation. All the mathematics, all the accumulations of the ages had availed for nothing. Charley Huyck held the secret. It was in the stars, and not an astronomer could find it. But with the seventeenth hour came the turn of fortune. The professor was passing through the office. The door was open, and the same fitful wind which had played the original prank was now just as fitfully performing restitution. Williams noticed a piece of paper protruding from the back of the bookcase and fluttering in the breeze. He picked it up. The first words that he saw were in the handwriting of Charley Huyck. He read:

"In the last extremity—in the last phase when there is no longer any water on the earth; when even the oxygen of the atmospheric envelope has been reduced to a minimum—man, or whatever form of intelligence is then upon the earth, must go back to the laws which governed his forebears. Necessity must ever be the law of evolution. There will be no water upon the earth, but there will be an unlimited quantity elsewhere.

"By that time, for instance, the great planet, Jupiter, will be in just a convenient state for exploitation. Gaseous now, it will be, by that time, in just about the stage when the steam and water are condensing into ocean. Eons of millions of years away in the days of dire necessity. By that time the intelligence and consciousness of the earth will have grown equal to the task.

"It is a thing to laugh at (perhaps) just at present. But when we consider the ratio of man's advance in the last hundred years, what will it be in a billion? Not all the laws of the universe have been discovered, by any means. At present we know nothing. Who can tell?

"Aye, who can tell? Perhaps we ourselves have in store the fate we would mete out to another. We have a very dangerous neighbor close beside us. Mars is in dire straits for water. And we know there is life on Mars and intelligence! The very fact on its face proclaims it. The oceans have dried up; the only way they have of holding life is by bringing their water from the polar snow-caps. Their canals pronounce an advanced state of cooperative intelligence; there is life upon Mars and in an advanced stage of evolution.

"But how far advanced? It is a small planet, and consequently eons of ages in advance of the earth's evolution. In the nature of things Mars cooled off quickly, and life was possible there while the earth was yet a gaseous mass. She has gone to her maturity and into her retrogression; she is approaching her end. She has had less time to produce intelligence than intelligence will have—in the end—upon the earth.

"How far has this intelligence progressed? That is the question. Nature is a slow worker. It took eons of ages to put life upon the earth; it took eons of more ages to make this life conscious. How far will it go? How far has it gone on Mars?"

That was as far the the comments went. The professor dropped his eyes to the rest of the paper. It was a map of the face of Mars, and across its center was a black cross scratched by the dull point of a soft pencil.

He knew the face of Mars. It was the Ascræus Lucus. The oasis at the juncture of a series of canals running much like the spokes of a wheel. The great Uranian and Alander Canals coming in at about right angles.

In two jumps the professor was in the observatory with the great lens swung to focus. It was the great moment out of his lifetime, and the strangest and most eager moment, perhaps, ever lived by any astronomer. His fingers fairly twitched with tension. There before his view was the full face of our Martian neighbor!

But was it? He gasped out a breath of startled exclamation. Was it Mars that he gazed at; the whole face, the whole thing had been changed before him.

Mars has ever been red. Viewed through the telescope it has had the most beautiful tinge imaginable, red ochre, the weird tinge of the desert in sunset. The color of enchantment and of hell!

For it is so. We know that for ages and ages the planet has been burning up; that life was possible only in the dry sea-bottoms and under irrigation. The rest, where the continents once were, was blazing desert. The redness, the beauty, the enchantment that we so admired was burning hell.

All this had changed.

Instead of this was a beautiful shade of iridescent green. The red was gone forever. The great planet standing in the heavens had grown into infinite glory. Like the great Dog Star transplanted.

The professor sought out the Ascræus Lucus. It was hard to find. The whole face had been transfigured; where had been canals was now the beautiful sheen of green and verdure. He realized what he was beholding and what he had never dreamed of seeing; the seas of Mars filled up.

With the stolen oceans our grim neighbor had come back to youth. But how had it been done. It was horror for our world. The great luminescent ball of Opalescence! Europe frozen and New York a mass of ice. It was the earth's destruction. How long could the thing keep up; and whence did it come? What was it?

He sought for the Ascræus Lucus. And he beheld a strange sight. At the very spot where should have been the juncture of the canals he caught what at first looked like a pin-point flame, a strange twinkling light with flitting glow of Opalescence. He watched it, and he wondered. It seemed to the professor to grow; and he noticed that the green about it was of different color. It was winking, like a great force, and much as if alive; baneful.

It was what Charley Huyck had seen. The professor thought of Charley. He had hurried to the mountain. What could Huyck, a mere man, do against a thing like this? There was naught to do but sit and watch it drink of our life-blood. And then—

It was the message, the strange assurance that Huyck was flashing over the world. There was no lack of confidence in the words he was speaking. "Celestial Kinetics," so that was the answer! Certainly it must be so with the truth before him. Williams was a doubter no longer. And Charley Huyck could save them. The man he had humored. Eagerly he waited and stuck by the lens. The whole world waited.

It was perhaps the most terrific moment since creation. To describe it would be like describing doomsday. We all of us went through it, and we all of us thought the end had come; that the earth was torn to atoms and to chaos.

The State of Colorado was lurid with a red light of terror; for a thousand miles the flame shot above the earth and into space. If ever spirit went out in glory that spirit was Charley Huyck! He had come to the moment and to Archimedes. The whole world rocked to the recoil. Compared to it the mightiest earthquake was but a tender shiver. The consciousness of the earth had spoken!

The professor was knocked upon the floor. He knew not what had happened. Out of the windows and to the north the flame of Colorado, like the whole world going up. It was the last moment. But he was a scientist to the end. He had sprained his ankle and his face was bleeding; but for all that he struggled, fought his way to the telescope. And he saw:

The great planet with its sinister, baleful, wicked light in the center, and another light vastly larger covering up half of Mars. What was it? It was moving. The truth set him almost to shouting.

It was the answer of Charley Huyck and of the world. The light grew smaller, smaller, and almost to a pin-point on its way to Mars.

The real climax was in silence. And of all the world only

Professor Williams beheld it. The two lights coalesced and spread out; what it was on Mars, of course, we do not know.

But in a few moments all was gone. Only the green of the Martian Sea winked in the sunlight. The luminous opal was gone from the Sargasso. The ocean lay in peace.

It was a terrible three days. Had it not been for the work of Robold and Huyck life would have been destroyed. The pity of it that all of their discoveries have gone with them. Not even Charley realized how terrific the force he was about to loosen.

He had carefully locked everything in vaults for a safe delivery to man. He had expected death, but not the cataclysm. The whole of Mount Robold was shorn away; in its place we have a lake fifty miles in diameter.

So much for celestial kinetics.

And we look to a green and beautiful Mars. We hold no enmity. It was but the law of self-preservation. Let us hope they have enough water; and that their seas will hold. We don't blame them, and we don't blame ourselves, either for that matter. We need what we have, and we hope to keep it.

In The ABYSS

~ By H. G. Wells ~

To this he was being towed, as a balloon might be towed by men out of the open country into a town. He approached it very slowly, and very slowly the dim irradiation was gathered together into more definite shapes.

Introduction

SCIENCE informs us that all life originally came from the sea, whether plant life or animal life, all had its origin in the waters of the ocean. Man's ancestry can readily be traced back to the fish, from our spinal column to our hair. Hair, science teaches us, is nothing but a modified fish scale. The thought that intelligent thinking beings could live at the bottom of the ocean should, therefore, not be scoffed at. It is this theme that our famous author has chosen in this fascinating tale, which you will follow with breathless interest down to the last word.

IN THE ABYSS

By H. G. Wells

A Five-Mile Descent Into the Ocean

THE lieutenant stood in front of the steel sphere and gnawed a piece of pine splinter. "What do you think of it, Steevens?" he said.

"It's an idea," said Steevens, in the tone of one who keeps an open mind.

"I believe it will smash—flat," said the lieutenant.

"He seems to have calculated it all out pretty well," said Steevens, still impartial.

"But think of the pressure," said the lieutenant. "At the surface of the water it's fourteen pounds to the inch, thirty feet down it's double that; sixty, treble; ninety, four times; nine hundred, forty times; five thousand, three hundred—that's a mile—it's two hundred and forty times fourteen pounds; that's—let's see—thirty hundredweight—a ton and a half, Steevens; a ton and a half to the square inch. And the ocean where he's going is five miles deep. That's seven and a half—"

"Sounds a lot," said Steevens, "but it's jolly thick steel."

The lieutenant made no answer, but resumed his pine splinter. The object of their conversation was a huge ball of steel, having an exterior diameter of perhaps nine feet. It looked like the shot for some Titanic piece of artillery. It was elaborately nested in a monstrous scaffolding built into the framework of the vessel, and the gigantic spars that were presently to sling it overboard gave the stern of the ship an appearance that had raised the curiosity of every decent sailor who had sighted it, from the Pool of London to the Tropic of Capricorn. In two places, one above the other, the steel gave place to a couple of circular windows of enormously thick glass, and one of these, set in steel frame of great solidity, was now partially unscrewed. Both the men had seen the interior of this globe for the first time that morning. It was elaborately padded with air cushions, with little studs sunk between bulging pillows to work the simple mechanism of the affair. Everything was elaborately padded, even the Myers apparatus which was to absorb carbonic acid and replace the oxygen inspired by its tenant, when he had crept in by the glass manhole, and had been screwed in. It was so elaborately padded that a man might have been fired from a gun in it with perfect safety. And it had need to be, for presently a man was to crawl in through that glass manhole, to be screwed up tightly, and to be flung overboard, and to sink down—down—down, for five miles, even as the lieutenant said. It had taken the strongest hold of his imagination; it made him a bore at mess; and he found Steevens the new arrival aboard, a godsend to talk to about it, over and over again.

"It's my opinion," said the lieutenant, "that, that glass will simply bend in and bulge and smash, under a pressure of that sort. Daubree has made rocks run like water under big pressures—and you mark my words—"

"If the glass did break in," said Steevens, "what then?"

"The water would shoot in like a jet of iron. Have you ever felt a straight jet of high pressure water? It would hit as hard as a bullet. It would simply smash him and flatten him. It would tear down his throat, and into his lungs; it would blow in his ears—"

"What a detailed imagination you have!" protested Steevens, who saw things vividly.

"It's a simple statement of the inevitable," said the lieutenant.

"And the globe?"

"Would just give out a few little bubbles, and it would settle down comfortably against the Day of Judgment, among the oozes and the bottom clay—with poor Elstead spread over his own smashed cushions like butter over bread."

He repeated this sentence as though he liked it very much. "Like butter over bread," he said.

"Having a look at the jigger?" said a voice, and Elstead stood behind them, spick and span in white, with a cigarette between his teeth, and his eyes smiling out of the shadow of his ample hat-brim. "What's that about bread and butter, Weybridge? Grumbling as usual about the insufficient pay of naval officers? It won't be more than a day now before I start. We are to get the slings ready to-day. This clean sky and gentle swell is just the kind of thing for swinging off a dozen tons of lead and iron, isn't it?"

"It won't affect you much," said Weybridge.

"No. Seventy or eighty feet down, and I shall be there

in a dozen seconds, there's not a particle moving, though the wind shriek itself hoarse up above, and the water lifts halfway to the clouds. No. Down there—" He moved to the side of the ship and the other two followed him. All three leant forward on their elbows and stared down into the yellow-green water.

A Description of the Apparatus

"But," said Elstead, finishing his thought aloud. "Are you dead certain that clockwork will act?" asked Weybridge presently.

"It has worked thirty-five times," said Elstead. "It's bound to work."

"But if it doesn't?"

"Why shouldn't it?"

"I wouldn't go down in that confounded thing," said Weybridge, "for twenty thousand pounds."

"Cheerful chap you are," said Elstead, and spat sociably at a bubble below.

"I don't understand yet how you mean to work the thing," said Steevens.

"In the first place, I'm screwed into the sphere," said Elstead, "and when I've turned the electric light off on three times to show I'm cheerful, I'm swung out over the stern by that crane, with all those big lead sinkers slung below me. The top lead weight has a roller carrying a hundred fathoms of strong cord rolled up, and that's all that joins the sinkers to the sphere, except the slings that will be cut when the affair is dropped. We use cord rather than wire rope because it's easier to cut and more buoyant—necessary points, as you will see.

"Through each of these lead weights you notice there is a

hole, and an iron rod will be run through that and will project six feet on the lower side. If that rod is rammed up from below, it knocks up a lever and sets the clockwork in motion at the side of the cylinder on which the cord winds.

"Very well. The whole affair is lowered gently into the water, and the slings are cut. The sphere floats—, with the air in it, it's lighter than water—, but the lead weights go down straight and the cord runs out. When the cord is all paid out, the sphere will go down too, pulled down by the cord."

"But why the cord?" asked Steevens. "Why not fasten the weights directly to the sphere?"

"Because of the smash down below. The whole affair will go rushing down, mile after mile, at a headlong pace at last. It would be knocked to pieces on the bottom if it wasn't for that cord. But the weights will hit the bottom, and directly they do, the buoyancy of the sphere will come into play. It will go on sinking slower and slower; come to stop at last, and then begin to float upward again.

"That's where the clockwork comes in. Directly the weights smash against the sea bottom, the rod will be knocked through and will kick up the clockwork, and the cord will be rewound on the reel. I shall be lugged down to the sea bottom. There I shall stay for half an hour, with the electric light on, looking about me. Then the clockwork will release a spring knife, the cord will be cut, and up I shall rush again, like a soda-water bubble. The cord itself will help the flotation."

"And if you should chance to hit a ship?" said Weybridge.

"I should come up at such a pace, I should go clean through it," said Elstead, "like a cannon ball. You needn't worry about that."

"And suppose some nimble crustacean should wriggle into your clockwork—"

"It would be a pressing sort of invitation for me to stop," said Elstead, turning his back on the water and staring at the sphere.

Starting the Descent

They had swung Elstead overboard by eleven o'clock. The day was serenely bright and calm, with the horizon lost in haze. The electric glare in the little upper compartment beamed cheerfully three times. Then they let him down slowly to the surface of the water, and a sailor in the stern chains hung ready to cut the tackle that held the lead weights and the sphere together. The globe, which had looked so large on deck, looked the smallest thing conceivable under the stern of the ship. It rolled a little, and its two dark windows, which floated uppermost, seemed like eyes turned up in round wonderment at the people who crowded the rail. A voice wondered how Elstead liked the rolling. "Are you ready?" sang out the commander. "Ay, ay, sir!" "Then let her go!"

The rope of the tackle tightened against the blade and was cut, and an eddy rolled over the globe in a grotesquely helpless fashion. Someone waved a handkerchief, someone else tried an ineffectual cheer, a middy was counting slowly, "Eight, nine, ten!" Another roll, then a jerk and a splash the thing righted itself.

It seemed to be stationary for a moment, to grow rapidly smaller, and then the water closed over it, and it became visible, enlarged by refraction and dimmer, below the surface. Before one could count three it had disappeared. There was a flicker of white light far down in the water, that diminished to a speck and vanished. Then there was nothing but a depth of water going down into blackness, through which a shark was swimming.

Then suddenly the screw of the cruiser began to rotate, the water was crickled, the shark disappeared in a wrinkled confusion, and a torrent of foam rushed across the crystalline clearness that had swallowed up Elstead. "What's the idea?" said one A.B. to another.

"We're going to lay off about a couple of miles, 'fear he should hit us when he comes up," said his mate.

The ship steamed slowly to her new position. Aboard her almost everyone who was unoccupied remained watching the breathing swell into which the sphere had sunk. For the next half-hour it is doubtful if a word was spoken that did not bear directly or indirectly on Elstead. The December sun was now high in the sky, and the heat very considerable.

"He'll be cold enough down there," said Weybridge. "They say that below a certain depth sea water's always just about freezing."

"Where'll he come up?" asked Steevens. "I've lost my bearings."

"That's the spot," said the commander, who prided himself on his omniscience. He extended a precise finger south-eastward. "And this, I reckon, is pretty nearly the moment," he said. "He's been thirty-five minutes."

"How long does it take to reach the bottom of the ocean?" asked Steevens.

"For a depth of five miles, and reckoning—as we did—an acceleration of two feet per second, both ways, is just about three-quarters of a minute."

Suspense and Waiting

"Then he's overdue," said Weybridge.

"Pretty nearly," said the commander. "I suppose it takes a few minutes for that cord of his to wind in."

"I forgot that," said Weybridge, evidently relieved.

And then began the suspense. A minute slowly dragged itself out, and no sphere shot out of the water. Another followed, and nothing broke the low oily swell. The sailors explained to one another that little point about the winding-in of the cord. The rigging was dotted with expectant faces. "Come up, Elstead!" called one hairy-chested salt impatiently, and the others caught it up, and shouted as though they were waiting for the curtain of a theatre to rise.

The commander glanced irritably at them.

"Of course, if the acceleration's less than two," he said, "he'll be all the longer. We aren't absolutely certain that was the proper figure. I'm no slavish believer in calculations."

Steevens agreed concisely. No one on the quarter-deck spoke for a couple of minutes. Then Steevens' watchcase clicked.

When, twenty-one minutes after the sun reached the zenith, they were still waiting for the globe to reappear, and not a man aboard had dared to whisper that hope was dead. It was Weybridge who first gave expression to that realisation. He spoke while the sound of eight bells still hung in the air. "I always distrusted that window," he said quite suddenly to Steevens.

"Good God!" said Steevens; "you don't think—?"

"Well!" said Weybridge, and left the rest to his imagination.

"I'm no great believer in calculations myself," said the commander dubiously, "so that I'm not altogether hopeless yet." And at midnight the gunboat was steaming slowly in a spiral round the spot where the globe had sunk, and the white beam of the electric light fled and halted and swept discontentedly onward again over the waste of phosphorescent waters under the little stars.

"If his window hasn't burst and smashed him," said Weybridge, "then it's a cursed sight worse, for his clockwork has gone wrong, and he's alive now, five miles under our feet, down there in the cold and dark, anchored in that little bubble of his, where never a ray of light has shone or a human being lived, since the waters were gathered together. He's there without food, feeling hungry and thirsty and scared, wondering whether he'll starve or stifle. Which will it be? The Myers apparatus is running out, I suppose. How long do they last?"

"Good heavens!" he exclaimed; "What little things we are! What daring little devils! Down there, miles and miles of water—all water, and all this empty water about us and this sky. Gulfs!" He threw his hands out, and as he did so, a little white streak swept noiselessly up the sky, travelled more slowly, stopped, became a motionless dot, as though a new star had fallen up into the sky. Then it went sliding back again and lost itself amidst the reflections of the stars and the white haze of the sea's phosphorescence.

A Slow Recovery

At the sight he stopped, arm extended and mouth open. He shut his mouth, opened it again, and waved his arms with an impatient gesture. Then he turned, shouted "Elstead ahoy!" to the first watch, and went at a run to Lindley and the search-light. "I saw him," he said "Starboard there! His light's on, and he's just shot out of the water. Bring the light round. We ought to see him drifting, when he lifts on the swell."

But they never picked up the explorer until dawn. Then they

almost ran him down. The crane was swung out and a boat's crew hooked the chain to the sphere. When they had shipped the sphere, they unscrewed the manhole and peered into the darkness of the interior (for the electric light chamber was intended to illuminate the water about the sphere, and was shut off entirely from its general cavity).

The air was very hot within the cavity, and the indiarubber at the lip of the manhole was soft. There was no answer to their eager questions and no sound of movement within. Elstead seemed to be lying motionless, crumpled in the bottom of the globe. The ship's doctor crawled in and lifted him out to the men outside. For a moment or so they did not know whether Elstead was alive or dead. His face, in the yellow light of the ship's lamps, glistened with perspiration. They carried him down to his own cabin.

He was not dead, they found, but in a state of absolute nervous collapse, and besides cruelly bruised. For some days he had to lie perfectly still. It was a week before he could tell his experiences.

Almost his first words were that he was going down again. The sphere would have to be altered, he said, in order to allow him to throw off the cord if need be, and that was all. He had, had the most marvellous experience. "You thought I should find nothing but ooze," he said. "You laughed at my explorations, and I've discovered a new world!" He told his story in disconnected fragments, and chiefly from the wrong end, so that it is impossible to re-tell it in his words. But what follows is the narrative of his experience.

Describing His Experience

It began atrociously, he said. Before the cord ran out, the thing kept rolling over. He felt like a frog in a football. He could see nothing but the crane and the sky overhead, with an occasional glimpse of people on the ships rail. He couldn't tell a bit which way the thing would roll next. Suddenly he would find his footing going up, and try to step, and over he went rolling, head over heels, and just anyhow, on the padding. Any other shape would have been more comfortable, but no other shape was to be relied upon under the huge pressure of the nethermost abyss.

Suddenly the swaying ceased; the globe righted, and when he had picked himself up, he saw the water all about him greeny-blue, with an attenuated light filtering down from above, and a shoal of little floating things went rushing up past him, as it seemed to him, towards the light. And even as he looked, it grew darker and darker, until the water above was as dark as the midnight sky, albeit of greener shade, and the water below black. And little transparent things in the water developed a faint glint of luminosity, and shot past him in faint greenish streaks.

And the feeling of falling! It was just like the start of a lift, he said, only it kept on. One has to imagine what that means, that keeping on. It was then of all times that Elstead repented of his adventure. He saw the chances against him in an altogether new light. He thought of the big cuttle-fish people knew to exist in the middle waters, the kind of things they find half digested in whales at times, or floating dead and rotten and half eaten by fish. Suppose one caught hold and wouldn't let go. And had the clockwork really been sufficiently tested? But whether he wanted to go on or go back mattered not the slightest now.

In fifty seconds everything was as black as night outside, except where the beam from his light struck through the waters, and picked out every now and then some fish or scrap of sinking matter. They flashed by too fast for him to see what they were. Once he thinks he passed a shark. And then the sphere began to get hot by friction against the water. They had underestimated this, it seems.

The first thing he noticed was that he was perspiring, and then he heard a hissing growing louder under his feet, and saw a lot of little bubbles—very little bubbles they were—rushing upward like a fan through the water outside. Steam! He felt the window, and it was hot. He turned on the minute glow-lamp that lit his own cavity, looked at the padded watch by the studs, and saw he had been travelling now for two minutes. It came into his head that the window would crack through the conflict of temperatures, for he knew the bottom water is very near freezing.

Then suddenly the floor of the sphere seemed to press against his feet, the rush of bubbles outside grew slower and slower, and the hissing diminished. The sphere rolled a little. The window had not cracked, nothing had given, and he knew that the dangers of sinking, at any rate, were over.

In another minute or so he would be on the floor of the abyss. He thought, he said, of Steevens and Weybridge and the rest of them five miles overhead, higher to him than the highest clouds that ever floated over land are to us, steaming slowly and staring down and wondering what had happened to him.

He peered out of the window. There were no more bubbles now, and the hissing had stopped. Outside there was a heavy blackness—as black as black velvet—except where the electric light pierced the empty water and showed the colour of it—a yellow-green. Then three things like shapes of fire swam into sight, following each other through the water. Whether they were little and near or big and far off he could not tell.

Each was outlined in a bluish light almost as bright as the lights of a fishing smack, a light which seemed to be smoking greatly, and all along the sides of them were specks of this, like the lighter portholes of a ship. Their phosphorescence seemed to go out as they came into the radiance of his lamp, and he saw then that they were little fish of some strange sort, with huge heads, vast eyes, and dwindling bodies and tails. Their eyes were turned towards him, and he judged they were following him down. He supposed they were attracted by his glare.

Presently others of the same sort joined them. As he went on down, he noticed that the water became of a pallid colour, and that little specks twinkled in his ray like motes in a sunbeam. This was probably due to the clouds of ooze and mud that the impact of his leaden sinkers had disturbed.

By the time he was drawn down to the lead weights he was in a dense fog of white that his electric light failed altogether to pierce for more than a few yards, and many minutes elapsed before the hanging sheets of sediment subsided to any extent. Then, lit by his light and by the transient phosphorescence of a distant shoal of fishes, he was able to see under the huge blackness of the super-incumbent water an undulating expanse of greyish-white ooze, broken here and there by tangled thickets of a growth of sea lilies, waving hungry tentacles in the air.

Farther away were the graceful, translucent outlines of a group of gigantic sponges. About this floor there were scattered a number of bristling flattish tufts of rich purple and black, which he decided must be some sort of sea-urchin, and small, large-eyed or blind things having a curious resemblance, some to woodlice, and others to lobsters, crawled sluggishly across the track of the light and vanished into the obscurity again, leaving furrowed trails behind them.

Then suddenly the hovering swarm of little fishes veered about and came towards him as a flight of starlings might do. They passed over him like a phosphorescent snow, and then he saw behind them some larger creature advancing towards the sphere.

An Unknown Creature of the Abyss

At first he could see it only dimly, a faintly moving figure remotely suggestive of a walking man, and then it came into the spray of light that the lamp shot out. As the glare struck it, it shut its eyes, dazzled. He stared in rigid astonishment.

It was a strange vertebrated animal. Its dark purple head was dimly suggestive of a chameleon, but it had such a high forehead and such a braincase as no reptile ever displayed before; the vertical pitch of its face gave it a most extraordinary resemblance to a human being.

Two large and protruding eyes projected from sockets in chameleon fashion, and it had a broad reptilian mouth with horny lips beneath its little nostrils. In the position of the ears were two huge gill-covers, and out of these floated a branching tree of coralline filaments, almost like the tree-like gills that very young rays and sharks possess.

But the humanity of the face was not the most extraordinary thing about the creature. It was a biped; its almost globular body was poised on a tripod of two frog-like legs and a long thick tail, and its fore limbs, which grotesquely caricatured the human hand, much as a frog's do, carried a long shaft of bone, tipped with copper. The colour of the creature was variegated; its head, hands and legs were purple; but its skin, which hung loosely upon it, even as clothes might do, was a phosphorescent grey. And it stood there blinded by the light.

At last this unknown creature of the abyss blinked its eyes open, and shading them with its disengaged hand, opened its mouth and gave vent to a shouting noise, articulate almost as speech might be, that penetrated even the steel case and padded jacket of the sphere. How a shouting may be accomplished without lungs Elstead does not profess to explain. It then moved sideways out of the glare into the mystery of shadow that bordered it on either side, and Elstead felt rather than saw that it was coming towards him. Fancying the light had attracted it, he turned the switch that cut off the current. In another moment something soft dabbed upon the steel, and the globe swayed.

Then the shouting was repeated, and it seemed to him that a distant echo answered it. The dabbing recurred, and the whole globe swayed and ground against the spindle over which the wire was rolled. He stood in the blackness and peered out into the everlasting night of the abyss. And presently he saw, very faint and remote, other phosphorescent quasi-human forms hurrying towards him.

Hardly knowing what he did, he felt about in his swaying prison for the stud of the exterior electric light, and came by accident against his own small glow-lamp in its padded recess. The sphere twisted, and then threw him down; he heard shouts like shouts of surprise, and when he rose to his feet, he saw two pairs of stalked eyes peering into the lower window and reflecting his light.

More Strange Experiences

In another moment hands were dabbing vigorously at his steel casing, and there was a sound, horrible enough in his position, of the metal protection of the clockwork being vigorously hammered. That indeed sent his heart into his mouth, for if these strange creatures succeeded in stopping that, his release would never occur. Scarcely had he thought as much when he felt the sphere sway violently, and the floor of it press hard against his feet. He turned off the small glow-lamp that lit the interior, and sent the ray of the large light in the separate compartment, out into the water. The sea-floor and the man-like creatures had disappeared, and a couple of fish chasing each other dropped suddenly by the window.

He thought at once that these strange denizens of the deep sea had broke the rope, and that he had escaped. He drove up faster and faster, and then stopped with a jerk that sent him flying against the padded roof of his prison. For half a minute perhaps, he was too astonished to think.

Then he felt that the sphere was spinning slowly, and rocking, and it seemed to him that it was also being drawn through the water. By crouching close to the window, he managed to make his weight effective and roll that part of the sphere downward, but he could see nothing save the pale ray of his light striking down ineffectively into the darkness. It occurred to him that he would see more if he turned the lamp off, and allowed his eyes to grow accustomed to the profound obscurity.

In this he was wise. After some minutes the velvety blackness became a translucent blackness, and then, far away, and as faint as zodiacal light of an English summer evening, he saw shapes moving below. He judged these creatures had detached his cable, and were towing him along the sea bottom.

And then he saw something faint and remote across the undulations of the submarine plain, a broad horizon of pale luminosity that extended this way and that way as far as the range of his little window permitted him to see. To this he was being towed, as a balloon might be towed by men out of the open country into a town. He approached it very slowly, and very slowly the dim irradiation was gathered together into more definite shapes.

It was nearly five o'clock before he came over this luminous area, and by that time he could make out an arrangement suggestive of streets and houses grouped about a vast roofless erection that was grotesquely suggestive of a ruined abbey. It was spread out like a map below him. The houses were all roofless enclosures of walls, and their substance being, as he afterwards saw, of phosphorescent bones, gave the place an appearance as if it were built of drowned moonshine.

Among the inner caves of the place waving trees of crinoid stretched their tentacles, and tall, slender, glassy sponges shot like shining minarets and lilies of filmy light out of the general glow of the city. In the open spaces of the place he could see a stirring movement as of crowds of people, but he was too many fathoms above them to distinguish the individuals in those crowds.

A City of the Abyss and Its People; the Explorer's End

Then slowly they pulled him down, and as they did so, the details of the place crept slowly upon his apprehension. He saw that the courses of the cloudy buildings were marked out with beaded lines of round objects, and then he perceived that at several points below him, in broad open spaces, were forms like the encrusted shapes of ships.

Slowly and surely he was drawn down, and the forms below him became brighter, clearer, more distinct. He was being pulled down, he perceived, towards the large building in the centre of the town, and he could catch a glimpse ever and again of the multitudinous forms that were lugging at his cord. He was astonished to see that the rigging of one of the ships, which formed such a prominent feature of the place, was crowded with a host of gesticulating figures regarding him, and then the walls of the great building rose about him silently, and hid the city from his eyes.

And such walls they were, of water-logged wood, and twisted wire-rope, and iron spars, and copper, and the bones and skulls of dead men. The skulls ran in zigzag lines and spirals and fantastic curves over the building; and in and out of their eye-sockets, and over the whole surface of the place, lurked and played a multitude of silvery little fishes.

Suddenly his ears were filled with a low shouting and a noise like the violent blowing of horns, and this gave place to a fantastic chant. Down the sphere sank, past the huge pointed windows, through which he saw vaguely a great number of these strange, ghostlike people regarding him, and at last he came to rest, as it seemed, on a kind of altar that stood in the centre of the place.

And now he was at such a level that he could see these strange people of the abyss plainly once more. To his astonishment, he perceived that they were prostrating themselves before him, all save one, dressed as it seemed in a robe of placoid scales, and crowned with a luminous diadem, who stood with his reptilian mouth opening and shutting, as though he led the chanting of the worshippers.

A curious impulse made Elstead turn on his small glow-lamp again, so that he became visible to these creatures of the abyss, albeit the glare made them disappear forthwith into night. At this sudden sight of him, the chanting gave place to a tumult of exultant shouts; and Elstead, being anxious to watch them, turned his light off again, and vanished from before their eyes. But for a time he was too blind to make out what they were doing, and when at last he could distinguish them, they were kneeling again. And thus they continued worshipping him, without rest or intermission, for a space of three hours.

Most circumstantial was Elstead's account of this astounding city and its people, these people of perpetual night, who have never seen sun or moon or stars, green vegetation, nor any living, air-breathing creatures, who know nothing of fire, nor any light but the phosphorescent light of living things.

Startling as is his story, it is yet more startling to find that scientific men, of such eminence as Adams and Jenkins, find nothing incredible in it. They tell me they see no reason why intelligent, water-breathing, vertebrated creatures, inured to a low temperature and enormous pressure, and of such a heavy structure, that neither alive nor dead would they float, might not live upon the bottom of the deep sea, and quite unsuspected by us, descendants like ourselves of the great Theriomorpha of the New Red Sandstone age.

We should be known to them however, as strange, meteoric creatures, wont to fall catastrophically dead out of the mysterious blackness of their watery sky. And not only we ourselves, but our ships, our metals, our appliances, would come raining down out of the night. Sometimes sinking things would smite down and crush them, as if it were the judgment of some unseen power above, and sometimes would come things of utmost rarity or utility, or shapes of inspiring suggestion. One can understand, perhaps, something of their behaviour at the descent of a living man, if one thinks what a barbaric people might do, to whom an enhaloed, shining creature came suddenly out of the sky.

At one time or another Elstead probably told the officers of the 'Ptarmigan' every detail of his strange twelve hours in the abyss. That he also intended to write them down is certain, but he never did, and so unhappily we have to piece together the discrepant fragments of his story from the reminiscences of Commander Simmons, Weybridge, Steevens, Lindley, and the others.

We see the thing darkly in fragmentary glimpses—the huge ghostly building, the bowing, chanting people, with their dark chameleon-like heads and faintly luminous clothing, and Elstead, with his light turned on again, vainly trying to convey to their minds that the cord by which the sphere was held was to be severed. Minute after minute slipped away, and Elstead, looking at his watch, was horrified to find that he had oxygen only for four hours more. But the chant in his honour kept on as remorselessly as if it was the marching song of his approaching death.

The manner of his release he does not understand, but to judge by the end of cord that hung from the sphere, it had been cut through by rubbing against the edge of the altar. Abruptly the sphere rolled over, and he swept up, out of their world, as an ethereal creature clothed in a vacuum would sweep through our own atmosphere back to its native ether again. He must have torn out of their sight as a hydrogen bubble hastens upwards from our air. A strange ascension it must have seemed to them.

The sphere rushed up with even greater velocity than, when weighted with the lead sinkers, it had rushed down. It became exceedingly hot. It drove up with the windows uppermost, and he remembers the torrent of bubbles frothing against the glass. Every moment he expected this to fly. Then suddenly something like a huge wheel seemed to be released in his head, the padded compartment began spinning about him, and he fainted. His next recollection was of his cabin, and of the doctor's voice.

But that is the substance of the extraordinary story that Elstead related in fragments to the officers of the 'Ptarmigan'. He promised to write it all down at a later date. His mind was chiefly occupied with the improvement of his apparatus, which was effected at Rio.

It remains only to tell that on February 2, 1896, he made his second descent into the ocean abyss, with the improvements his first experience suggested. What happened we shall probably never knew. He never returned. The 'Ptarmigan' beat about over the point of his submersion, seeking him in vain for thirteen days. Then she returned to Rio, and the news was telegraphed to his friends. So the matter remains for the present. But it is hardly probable that no further attempt will be made to verify his strange story of these hitherto unsuspected cities of the deep sea.

"WHISPERING ETHER"

By Charles S. Wolfe

I point it right at his head, and makin' my voice as hard as I can I says, tense-like, "You speak one word and you'll eat your breakfast in hell." And Proctor smiles. Get that? With my gat aimed at his head he smiles. And, fellow, when Proctor smiles it gives you the creeps.

Introduction

AN amazing story by that versatile author, Mr. Wolfe. The ether is something we know nothing about. But its action and its waves give a basis for the strange mystery we are told of here. It touches on the world of ether waves which are appealing to our radio fans and while this of course in the realm of abstract science, we have again in this story the everyday crude thinker mystified by it all, and this is the history of the world. The intelligence of each of us is very limited, and our habits and ways of thought are only a little more clumsy than our author's characters, whom he uses to bring out as always a wonderful contrast. The story is well worth reading.

WHISPERING ETHER

By Charles S. Wolfe

I'M NOT a scientist. "Cans" is my line. Safes, you know. "Soup," nitro-glycerine, that kind of thing, get me? "Shoe-maker stick to your last." Them is my sentiments, and I stick to my own trade. But now that they got me tied up in this confounded jail, and I ain't got much to do with my spare time I got a notion to jot down what I know about that Proctor affair that you maybe read about in the papers. Reporters was after me thick when it happened, but I was the silent kid. It pays to keep your mouth shut in the circles I move in.

Proctor's in the bug house. Three alienists, or whatever you call those ginks that admit they're sane and prove you're not, pronounced him hopelessly insane. I ain't disputing no jury of my peers. If they say lie's a nut, he's a nut, that's all. But--I didn't get introduced to Proctor in the regular way. We didn't have no mutual acquaintances to slip us the knock-down. It all came about thru me droppin' in one night, casual like, to blow his safe. You might wonder what a yegg would want out of a laboratory safe. Maybe you'll wise up when I tip you it was a contract job. Not my own, see? I'm namin' no names, but there was a gang of big guys that wanted old Proctor's formula for Chero, and thought it would be cheaper to buy it off me than him. Anyway, I'm after the paper with the makeup of this explosive when I jimmied the laboratory window.

I'm sayin' this right here: Proctor may be a nut, but he's no boob. I was expecting burglar alarms. scientific thief traps, all that kind of stuff. And I was all fixt for an electrified box. Proctor put one over on me just the same. And if he didn't do it with the mind machine, how in Hell else do you account for it?

I was workin' on the old can. She was a fairly respectable affair, and I make up my mind to blow her. I was drillin' away when click goes a switch and the sudden flare of light dazzled me. Were you ever caught working on a guy's safe, brother? No? Well, take it from Oscar, it's like nothing you ever felt before.

Even before I can see right my mind's workin' overtime hunting for a way out. And then I can see again, and there stands Proctor, a long cord trailing behind him and 'phones over his ears like the wireless men. And I notice with joy that he ain't got a gat—not that I can see.

Anyway, I risk it. Just as quick as I can draw I flashes my automatic. I point it right at his head, . and makin' my voice as hard as I can I says, tense-like, "You speak one word and you'll eat your breakfast in Hell."

And Proctor smiles. Get that? With my gat at his head

he smiles. And, fellow, when Proctor smiles it gives you the creeps. And then he says—s' help me—I'm not bullyin' you—P-Put your gun away, it's not loaded."

Can you beat that? It wasn't either, but how did he know it? Bluffing? That's what I thought, and I sees his bet and raises him. "You move," I growls, "and you'll discover you're a bad guesser."

He smiles again. Say, I can feel my flesh creep yet. "It's not loaded," he says, very calm, and he walks a few steps toward me. I don't shoot. You can't, you know, with an empty gun, and I see that he's called my bluff.

"You win," I says. "It ain't. But I can beat the life out of you with it."

That smile again. His hand goes to his pocket. He pulls out a little bottle, just about the size they sell you pills in. "That, my friend," he says, "is full of Chero. If I just toss it at your feet, you'll never attempt to steal a formula again on this planet."

Does he win? He owns the building. "Call the officer," and I chucks the gun on the floor. "I'll go quietly."

"Sensible," he remarks; "very sensible. You possess judgment, even if you do lack courage. Who sent you here?"

"Call in the bulls," I growls. "I'm not squealing." He takes no notice. "I know who sent you. I knew you were coming."

"Look here," I blurts, "if that gang framed me, I'll talk. They sent for me, I didn't go to them. I—"

"No one informed me, if that's what you mean," he says, coldly. "It is not necessary for any one to inform me of anything. The world is an open book to me."

(That's just what he told that gang of saw-bones afterwards, and they said he was looney. But if they had seen him as I seen him—)

He was talking again. "My man," I wriggled when he

spoke, "the men for whom you work are imbeciles. I have named my price for Chero, and they don't want to pay it. They believe they can wrest it from me by force or trickery. You are their first emissary, and it is my wish that you be their last. I am going to. convince them that it is useless to attempt anything of the kind with me. I am not going to turn you over to the police. I am going to show you something, and then I am going to send you back to your masters to tell them what you have seen. After that," he smiled, "I don't think I shall be troubled by them. Come!"

He stalked into the next room, me at his heels. There wasn't much in that room—just a table covered with apparatus. I have seen a wireless set. It looked something like that, only—well there was something different about it.

He pointed to it. Oh! I can see him yet, with his flashing eyes, and his big dome. "There," says he, "is the mind machine. And you, a criminal, are the first man to see it except its creator."

I'm getting on my feet again, and not so scared, and so I gazes at it curious. "What is it, Doc?" I asks.

"It reads your thoughts," he says, just as solemn as an owl.

That's right, laugh. I don't blame you. I grinned myself. He saw me grin, and he turned on me like a tiger.

"Dolt," he hollers. "Clod! You doubt. Pig! Your type has retarded the progress of mankind throughout the ages. You sneer—you imbecile!" Well, just then I'm like the doctors. "A nut!" I thinks, "and loose with that bottle of Chero in his pocket!" And it's up to me to soothe him.

"How does it work?" I asks, to gain time. When you're in a room with a nut that's nursin' a bottle of H. E. your one thought is to go away from there. And this particular nut don't want me to. But I have hopes.

By dumb luck I hits the right chord. "How does it work?"

gets results. Right away he seems to forget he's mad. He seems to forget I'm a yegg. He gets kind of dreamy, and he runs a caressin' hand over the shiny brass of the nearest instrument. "Simple," he says, "very simple. It is based on the electro-magnetic wave and the conducting ether theories." It's over my head, but I listen. "Have you ever considered just what happens when you think intensely? By an effort of what you call the Will, you concentrate on what you are thinking. Emotion, too, plays its part. You are intensely angry, intensely worried, intensely interested. This concentrating acts physically on the brain. There is a call on the heart for more blood. And the heart responds, sending a thicker, faster stream to the affected locality. Now what happens?" He turns to me like my teacher used to do in school when there was a question to be answered.

"Search me," I murmurs.

But he doesn't even see me, I guess. "The increased stream, rushing at an unusual rate, rubs against the walls of the veins and arteries of the head, *producing friction.*"

"I see," I says, politely. But I don't.

"This friction is the physical result of the mental action. Your purely mental process has, by the membership of the rushing blood and its attending friction, been transformed into, or has produced, a physical manifestation."

His voice sank to a whisper. "It is this fact that makes my great invention possible. The friction set up produces faint currents of electricity. It is Nature's own generator. The currents are faint, weak, but they are there. And they vary in intensity in proportion as the rushing blood stream surges and ebbs. Thus they have imprinted on them all the characteristics of the thought that gives rise to them. They vary in the individual. Some minds can generate a current one hundred—yes, one thousand—times greater than others, but all minds generate to some extent.

"And these electrical impulses are thrown out into space in wave trains, exactly as the radio telegraph throws them out. This accounts for the phenomena of mental telepathy. If conditions are just right, the receiving mind in perfect tune with the transmitting mind, and sensitive enough to interpret the received impulses, you have accomplished telepathy. All that remained for me to do was to measure the intensity and characteristics of the generated current, its frequency—and it is high—and—"

He paused and fixt me with that fishy stare. I didn't know just what to say, so I took a Brody. "And what, Doc? Slip it to me quick."

"And the length of the emitted waver he comes back at me, triumphantly. "It might be one millionth of a meter or it might be one million meters. Or it might be any length between those extremes. Or beyond them, for that matter. I succeeded in making these measurements."

He laughed. Or, rather, he laughed and snarled all at once. I'm telling you straight, fellow, your hair stands on end when Proctor laughs like that. "I fancy-some of your radio experts would gape if they were permitted to see my wave meter. I believe it would cause some excitement in the laboratories of Lodge or Marconi. I—Proctor—I measured these waves which, of course, means that I found a detector for them. Our friend DeForest thinks , that he has a monopoly on ultra-sensitive detectors. Proctor's detector is to the audion what a stop watch is to a wheel barrow!

"And the frequency. It is beyond the limits of audibility, as that term is understood. I wound phones that will render the received signals audible. And the task was done."

Most of that stuff had gone over, but like a lightning flash the big idea burst thru' my shrapnel-proof cranium. I fairly stuttered as I got his drift. I'll bet my eyes popped as I gaped at that machine. "Good God!" I spluttered. "Do you mean that that thing can hear you think?"

Proctor smiled the nearest to a human smile that I ever saw on his mug. "You have glimmerings of intelligence," he paid, in a gratified way; "I mean just that."

And then he went off his handle again. "And I mean," he roared, "that you are to go back to the scum that sent you and tell them that it is useless for them to plot against me, for I can hear their very thoughts as they think them. I can read their miserable souls! That's how I knew you were coming here to-night! That's how I knew that your lethal weapon contained no charge! And," he seized me and shook me until my heels nearly broke my neck, "And that's how I know, you swine, that even now you don't know whether to believe me or not." He released me and tore the telephone things from off his ears. "Here!" he bellowed, clamping them over my ears, "here! Listen, and be convinced."

He wheeled to the table and whirled knobs and dials. A continuous humming and buzzing sounded in the 'phones.

And then it happened. Listen to me close. I know they labeled Proctor "squirrel food" for telling them less than this, but— This was *July of 1914*. Get that?

Suddenly something like a voice—no, not like a voice, either—like a voice inside my own head, if you can get me, said masterfully, *with a strong German accent, "Serbia will, because she dare not submit. France must, because she will see my mind behind it. England must* as a *last desperate effort to save herself. But my armies will grind them like grain in the mill. And then—"*

Proctor tore the 'phones from me. I was like a stuffed doll

and I never raised a mitt. He grabbed me, and it was just like being caught in the jaws of a vise. "You have heard," he thundered. "Now go"

The last thing I remember was that he heaved me toward the door. I remember spinning toward it. And that's all.

The next thing I remember is waking up in that hospital ward. It was July of 1914 when Proctor chucked me, and it was late August when I found myself in that hospital.

As near as I can learn I missed the door, hit the wall and a bottle of that Chero stuff got knocked off a shelf. They dug Proctor and I out of the ruins, and we were both pretty well messed up. Proctor raved about his ruined mind machine, and it got him a pass to the squirrel cage. .

If you read the papers at the, time you'll remember Proctor wanted me to back him up, but I wouldn't talk. Least said, easiest remedied.

Now you got all I know about it. I spilled it once to Gentleman Joe, a high-brewed crook, who soaked up all they pass you at Harvard when he was young. Joe said maybe Proctor fooled me with a camoflaged phonograph.

Maybe he did. I might think so myself if it had happened in *September* instead of *July*, 1914. Get me?*

(**Editor's note*. By September of that year, all three nations were at war with Germany's Kaiser.)

The EGGS from LAKE TANGANYIKA

By Curt Siodmak

Crying and screaming, the people fled from the street and crowded into the houses. They couldn't tell where the insect would fall, and they were afraid of their heads.

Introduction

WE consider this extraordinary story a classic, and certainly the best scientifiction story so far for 1926. How large can insects grow? Is there any limit to their size? Frankly, no one knows. We have almost microscopically small flies, and in some of the tropical countries we have some almost as large as the fist. Is it possible to have still larger flies, and could monstrous flies such as are depicted in this story, be bred at some future date? The author of this brilliant tale evidently thinks so. Anyway, we trust he is mistaken, as we should not like to meet such monsters. The science of entomology presented in this story is excellent, and will arouse your imagination.

THE EGGS FROM LAKE TANGANYIKA

By Curt Siodmak

PROFESSOR Meyer-Maier drew a sharp needle out of the cushion, carefully pinked up with the pincers the fly lying in front of him and stuck it carefully upon a piece of white paper. He looked over the rim of his glasses, dipped his pen in the ink and wrote under the specimen:

"*Glossina palpalis,* specimen from Tsetsefly River. In the aboriginal language termed *nsi-nsi* Usually found on river courses and lakes in West Africa. Bearer of the malady Negana (Tse-tse sickness—sleeping sickness.)"

He laid down the pen and took up a powerful magnifying glass for a closer examination. "A horrible creature," he murmured, and shivered involuntarily. On each side of the head of the flying horror, there was a monstrous eye surrounded by many sharp lashes and divided up into a hundred thousand flashing facets. An ugly proboscis thickly studded with curved barbs or hooks grew out of the lower side of the head. The wings were small and pointed, the legs armed with thorns, spines and claws. The thorax was muscular, like that of a prize fighter. The abdomen was thin and looked like India rubber. It could take in a great quantity of blood and expand like a balloon. On the whole, the flying horror, resembling a pre-historic flying dragon, was not very pleasant looking—Prof. Meyer-Maier took a pin and transfixed the body of the fly. It seemed to him that a vicious sheen of light emanated from the eyes and that the proboscis rolled up. Quickly he picked up the magnifying glass, but it was an optical illusion—the thing was dead, with all its poison still within its body.

Memories of the Expedition to Africa

WITH a deep sigh he laid aside pincers and magnifying glass and sank into a deep reverie. The clock struck 12, 1-2-3-4-5, counted Professor Meyer-Maier,

In Udjidji, a village on lake Tanganyika, the natives had told him of gigantic flies inhabiting the interior further north. These monsters were three times as big as the giants composing the giant bodyguard of the Prince of Ssuggi, who all had to be of at least standard height. Meyer-Maier laughed over this negro fable, but the negroes were obstinate. They refused to follow him to the northern part of Lake Tanganyika. Even Msu-uru, his black servant, who otherwise made an intelligent impression, trembled with excitement and begged to be left out of the expedition—because there enormous flies and bees were to be found,—that let no man approach. They drank the river dry and guarded the valley of the elephants. "The Valley of the Elephants" was a fabled place where the old pachyderms withdrew to die. "It is inexplicable," soliloquized Meyer-Maier, "that no one ever found a dead elephant." The clock struck 6-7-8.

The natives had come along on the expedition much against their will. Moyer-Maier had trouble to keep the caravan moving up to the day when he found four great, strange looking eggs, larger than ostrich eggs. The negroes were seized with a panic, half of them deserting in the night, in spite of the great distance from the coast. The other half could only be kept there by tremendous efforts. He had to make up his mind finally, to go back, but he secretly put the eggs he had found into his camping chest to solve their riddle.

Now they were here in his Berlin home, in his work-room. He had not found time as yet to examine them, for he had brought much material home to be worked over.

The clock struck 9-10.

Meyer-Maier kept thinking of the ugly head of the tse-tse fly that he had seen through the magnifying glass. A strange thought occurred to him and made him smile. Suppose the stories of the negroes were true and the giant flies—butterflies and beetles as big as elephants did exist! And suppose that they propagated as flies do!—each one laying eighty million eggs a year! He laughed aloud and pictured to himself how such a creature would stalk through the streets.

A Strange Sound and the Hatching of an Egg

HE broke off suddenly, in the midst of his laughter. A sound reached his ear, an earsplitting buzzing like that of a thousand flies, a deafening hum, as if a swarm of bees were entering the room; it burst out like a blast of wind through the room and then stopped. Meyer-Maier jerked the door open. Nothing. All was quiet. "I must relax for a while," said he, and opened the window. He turned on the light and threw back the lid of the big chest, which contained the giant eggs. Suddenly he grew pale as death and staggered back. A creature was crawling out, a creature as big as a police dog—a frightful creature, with wings —a muscular body, and six hairy legs with claws. It crept slowly, raised its incandescent head to the light and polished its wings with its hind legs. Faint with fright, Meyer-Maier pressed against the wall with outspread arms. A loud buzzing, — the creature swept across the room, climbed up on the window sill and was gone. Meyer-Maier came slowly to himself. "My nerves are deceiving me. Did I dream?" he whispered, and dragged himself to the camp-chest. But he became frozen with horror. One egg was broken open. "It breaks out of its shell like a chicken, it does not change into a chrysalis," he thought mechanically. At last his mind cleared and he awoke to the emergency. He sprang to the desk, snatched up his revolver, ran downstairs and out into the street, He saw no trace of the escaped giant insect. Meyer. Maier looked up at the lighted windows of his home. Suddenly the light became dim. "The other eggs "—like a blow came the thought—"the other eggs too have broken." He raced back up the stairs. A deafening buzzing filled the room. He jerked his door open and fired—once, twice, until the magazine was empty—the room was silent. Through the window he saw three silhouettes sweeping high across the night-sky and disappearing in the direction of the great woods in the West. In the chest there lay the four broken giant eggs

A Call for His Colleague

MEYER-MAIER sank upon a chair. "It's against all logic," he thought, and glanced at at the empty revolver in his hand. "My, delirium has taken wings and crawled out of the egg. What shall I do? Shall I call the police? They will send we to an alienist! Keep quiet about it? Look for the creatures? I'll call up my colleague, Schmidt-Schmitt!" He dragged himself to the telephone and got a connection. Schmidt-Schmitt was at home! "This is Meyer-Maier," sounded a tired voice. "Come over at once!"

"What's the trouble?" asked Schmidt-Schmitt. "My African giant eggs have burst," lisped Meyer-Maier with a failing voice. "You most come at once!"

"Your nerves are out of order," answered Schmidt-Schmitt. Have you still got the creatures?"

"They've gone," whispered Meyer-Maier,—he thought he would collapse,—"flew out of the window."

"There, there," laughed Schmidt-Schmitt. "Now, we are getting to the truth—of course they aren't there. Anyhow, I'll come over. Meanwhile take a cognac and put on a cold pack."

"Take your car, and say nothing about what I told you."

Professor Meyer-Maier hung up the receiver. It was incredible. He pressed his hand to his forehead. If the empty shells were not irrefutable evidence, he would have been inclined to think of hallucinations.

He helped himself to some brandy and after the second glass he felt better. "I wish Professor Schmidt-Schmitt would come. He ought to be here by now. He will have an explanation and will help me to get myself in hand again. The day of ghosts and miracles is long past. But why isn't he here? He ought to have come by this time." Meyer-Maier looked out of the window. A car came tearing through the dark street and stopped with squeaking brakes in front of Meyer-Maier's residence. A form jumped out like an india rubber ball, ran up the steps, burst into Meyer-Maiers' study, and collapsed into a chair.

"How awful," he gasped.

"It seems to me, you are even more excited over it than I," said Professor Meyer-Maier dispiritedly while he watched his shaking friend.

"Absolutely terrible" Professor Schmidt-Schmitt wiped his forehead with a silk handkerchief. "You were not suffering from nerves, you had no hallucinations. Just now I saw a fly-creature as large as a heifer falling upon a horse. The monster grew big and heavy, while the horse collapsed and the fly flew away. I examined the horse. Its veins and arteries were empty. Not a drop of blood was leftin its body. The driver fainted with fright and has not come to yet. It is a world catastrophe."

Notifying the Police

"WE must notify the police at once."

A quick telephone connection was obtained. The police Lieutenant in charge himself answered.

"This is Professor Meyer-Maier talking! Please believe what I am going to tell you. I am neither drunk nor crazy. Four poisonous gigantic flies, as large as horses are at large in the city. They must be destroyed at all costs."

"What are you trying to do? Kid me?" the lieutenant came back in an angry voice.

"Believe me—for God's sake," yelled Meyer-Maier,

reaching the end of his nervous strength. "Hold the wire." The Lieutenant turned to the desk of the sergeant. "What is up now?"

"A cab driver has been here who says that his horse was killed by a gigantic bird on Karlstrasse." "Get the men of the second platoon ready for immediate action" he ordered the sergeant, and turned back to the telephone. "Hello Professor! Are you still there? Please come over as quickly as possible. What you told me is true. One of these giant insects has been seen."

Professor Meyer-Maier hung up. He loaded his revolver and put a Browning pistol into his colleague's hand. "Is your car still downstairs?" "Yes I took the little limousine." "Excellent—then the monster cannot attack us." They rushed on through the night.

"What can happen. now?" inquired Professor Schmidt-Sshmitt.

"These giant flies may propagate and multiply in the manner of the housefly. And in that case, due to their strength and poisonous qualities" continued Professor Meyer-Maier, "the whole human race will perish in a few weeks. When they crept from the shell they were as large as dogs. They grew to the size of a horse within an hour. God knows what will happen next. Let as hope and pray that we will be able to find and kill the four flies and destroy the eggs which they have laid in the meantime, within fourteen days."

The car came to a stop in front of the Police Station. A policeman armed with steel helmet and hand trench bombs swinging from his belt tore open the limousine door. The lieutenant hastened out and conducted the scientists into the station house. "Any more news?" inquired Meyer-Maier.

"The West Precinct station just called up. One of their

patrolmen saw a giant animal fly over the Teutoburger Forest. Luckily we had war tanks near there which immediately net out in search of the creature."

The telephone-bell rang. The lieutenant rushed to the phone.

"Central Police Station."

"East Station talking. Report comes from Lake Wieler, that a gigantic fly has attacked two motor boats."

"Put small trench mortars on the police-boat and go out on the lake. Shoot when the beast gets near you."

The door of the Station-House opened and the city commissioner entered. "I have just heard some fabulous stories," he said, and approached the visitors. "Professor Meyer-Maier? Major PritzelWilzell! Can you explain all this?"

"I brought home with me four large eggs from my African expedition, for examination. Tonight these *eggs* broke open. Four great flies came out—a sort of tse-tse fly, such as is found on Lake Tanganyika. The creatures escaped through the window and we must make every endeavor to kill them at once."

The telephone bell rang as if possessed.

"This is the Central Broadcasting Station. A giant bird has been caught in the high voltage lines. It has fallen down and lies on the street."

"Close the street at once." The major took up the instrument. "Call up the Second Company. Let all four flying companies go off with munition and gasoline for three days. Come with me my friends, we will get at least one of them!"

An armored automobile came tearing along at a frightful speed. "We appreciate your foresight, Major," said Meyer-Maier, as they stepped into the steel-armored machine.

One of the Giant Flies Is Electrocuted

ALTHOUGH it was five o'clock in the morning, the square in front of the broadcasting station was black with people. The police kept a space clear in the center, where monstrously large and ugly, lay the dead giant fly. Its wings were burnt, its proboscis extended, while the legs, with their claws, were drawn up against the body. The abdomen was a great ball, full of bright red liquid. "That is certainly the creature that killed the horse," said Schmidt-Schimitt, and pointed at the thick abdomen. He then walked around the creature. "*Glossina palpalis*. A monstrous tse-tse fly." "Will you please send the monster to the zoological laboratory?" The major nodded assent. The firemen, prepared for service, pushed poles under the insect and tried to lift it up from the ground. Out of the air came *a* droning sound. An airplane squadron dropped out of the clouds and again disappeared. A bright body with vibrating wings flew across the sky. The airplanes dropped on it. The noise of the machine-guns started. The bright body fell in a spiral course to the ground. Crying and screaming, the people fled from the street and crowded into the houses. They couldn't tell where the insect would fall and they were afraid of their heads. The street was empty in an instant. The body of the monster fell directly in front of the armored car and lay there, stiff. In its fall it carried away a lot of aerial cable and now it lay on the pavement as if caught in a net, the head• torn by the machine gun bullets. It looked like a strange gleaming cactus.

"Take me to my home, Major," groaned Meyer-Maier. "I can't stand it any longer. The excitement is too much for me."

In the Hospital

THE armored car started noisily into motion. Meyer-Maier fell from the seat, senseless, upon the floor of the tonneau. When he came to himself, he lay in a strange bed. His gaze fell upon a bell which swung to and fro above his face. In his head there was a humming like an airplane motor. He made no attempt, even to think. His finger pressed the push-button and he never released it until half-a-dozen attendants came rushing into the room. One figure stood out in dark colors, in the group of white-clad interns. It was his colleague, Schmidt-Schmitt.

"You're awake?" said he, and stepped to his bed. "How are you feeling?"

"My head is buzzing as if there were a swarm of hornets living in it. How many hours have I lain here?"

"Hours?" Schmidt-Schmitt dwelt upon the word. "Today is the fifteenth day that you are lying in Professor Stiebling's sanitorium. It was a difficult case. You always woke up at meal-time and without saying a word, went to sleep again."

"Fifteen days!" cried Meyer-Maier excitedly. "And the insects? Have they been killed?"

"I'll tell you the whole story when you are well again," said Schmidt-Schmitt, quieting him. "Lie as you are, quietly—any excitement may hurt you." "They must not come into the room!" he screamed out to an excited messenger, who breathlessly pulled the door open.

"Professor! —" the man was in deadly fear — "the Central Police station has given out the news that a swarm of giant flies are descending upon the city."

"Barricade all windows at once!"

"You wasted precious time," screamed Meyer-Maier, and jumped out of the bed. "Let me go to my house. I must solve the riddle as to how to get at the insects. Don't touch me," he raved. He snatched a coat from the rack, ran out of the house, and jumped into Schmidt-Schmitt's automobile which stood at the gate, and went like the wind, to his home. The door of his house was ajar. He rushed up four flights and in delirious haste rushed into his workroom. The telephone bell rang.

The Danger Is Over

MEYER-MAIER snatched up the receiver. He got the consoling message from the city police-commissioner: "The danger is over, Professor. Our air-squadron has destroyed the swarm with a cloud of poison-gas. Only two of the insects escaped death. These we have caught in a net and are taking them to the zoological gardens."

"And if they have left eggs behind them?"

"We are going to search the woods systematically and will inject Lysol into any eggs we find. I think that will help," laughed the Major. "Shall I send some of them to you for examination?"

"No," cried Meyer-Maier in fright. "Keep them off my neck."

He sat down at his work-table. There seemed a vicious smile on the face of the transfixed dead tsetse fly. "You frightful ghost," murmured the professor with pallid lips, and threw a book on the insect. His head was in a daze. He tried his best to think clearly. An axiom of science came to him: if the flies are as large as elephants, they can only progagate as fast as elephants do. They can't have a million young ones, but only a few. "I can't be wrong," he murmured. "I'll look up the confirmation."

He took up the telephone and called the city Commissioner.

"Major, how many insects were in the swarm?"

"Thirteen. Eleven are dead. The other two will never escape alive. They are fed up with the poison-gas."

"Thank you." Meyer-Maier hung up the receiver. "Very well," he murmured, "now there can be no question of any danger, for each fly can only lay the or four eggs at once—not a million."

An immense weariness overcame him. He went into his bed-room and fell exhausted on his bed. "It is well that there is a supreme wisdom which controls the laws of nature. Otherwise the world would be subject to the strangest surprises." He thought of the monsters and crept anxiously under the bed-clothes. I will entrust Schmidt-Schmitt with the investigation of the creature phenomenon, I simply can't stand further excitement."

And sleep spread the mantel of well-deserved quiet over him.

The TELEPATHIC PICK-UP

~ By Samuel M. Sargent, Jr. ~

There sounded a wild scream. Dr. Spaulding leaped upon the machine, gibbering incoherently, and smashed the mechanism into a thousand pieces.

Introduction

THIS gripping story—worthy of a Poe—is based in a degree, upon radio. A machine developed by the hero of the story, can be tuned into the wave-lengths of any given person's thoughts, thus giving the possessor a wonderful power. And this story, with its tragic termination, tells not only of the possibilities of radio in the future, but also touches on—and elaborates—the fantastic theory that the electric shock sustained by the human system while in the electric chair, does not really kill, but simply puts the victim into a state of unconsciousness with a temporary cessation of organic function. But this is not a mere scientific treatise on the possibilities of the future for radio or capital punishment, it is a story full of human interest, though not without a touch of the ghastly. Anyhow, you will be glad to have read it.

THE TELEPATHIC PICK-UP

By Samuel M. Sargent, Jr.

THERE was a strange light in Doctor Spaulding's eyes. His face was immobile, but the lines were set in an expression of jubilance and triumph. "Come on, Brant," he said quietly, "I have something interesting to show you."

With that remark, he wheeled, and strode into the gloom of the hall. I followed, and our footsteps echoed with hollowness in that spacious, blank space.

I had always felt a certain timidity when with Doctor Spaulding. We had been friends for years, and yet strangers. His was a personality which had seemingly been fashioned for dominance over me. I had never been able, in our long acquaintance, to raise my head squarely, and hold the gaze of his eyes. My fount of conversation dried up beneath the queer influence of him, and I was reserved and stumbling in my speech.

I admired, with no malice, his genius—his eccentric and versatile genius that had placed him at the head of his profession, had made him an eminent scientist, and had allowed him to conquer the field of electricity. He had performed, during his career, many marvelous feats of surgery, had made important advances in both astronomy and chemistry, and had given countless electrical inventions to the world. Of late years, he had devoted himself entirely to electrical research.

I had seen him but once in the last year and a half. At that meeting he had hinted to me that he was at work on a radio apparatus that would startle the world.

"It won't be called radio though, Brant," he had told me with a dry, rasping chuckle. "It shall have another name. When it is finished, I shall explain it all first to you."

So when I received his phone call I concluded that he had completed the invention, and I was burning with curiosity as I followed him down the hall.

He turned into the living room. That chamber was no darker, no emptier, and no more gloomy than any other room in his house, but I loathed it even more than the other. For always as I entered, I was brought face to face with a portrait of the doctor's brother, and the tragedy was forcibly recalled to me. It had been many years ago, but time had not dulled it in my friend's mind, nor my own. I could well remember that night, and Tom Spaulding's flight, a jump ahead of the law, because he was wanted for embezzlement of fifty thousand dollars. The disgrace of it had crushed the doctor, and because it was his beloved brother, the blow was even greater. It had aged and changed him, and sent him into the life of a recluse. That it was responsible for his many invaluable discoveries was probable, but not any less regrettable, at least to me. As for Tom Spaulding, we had not heard of him since that night, but perhaps that was just as well, for we learned later that he had sunk to the lowest level of the underworld.

I gave the picture as fleeting a glance as possible, but the doctor stood for a long while gazing up at it. He seemed lost in revery. At last he recovered himself with a start, motioned me to a chair, and turned to the huge mahogany table. He bent over a large, box-like cabinet of dark wood, like and yet unlike the ordinary radio set. He tinkered for a few minutes with the knobs and dials. Then he faced me again.

"This is the invention," he said. "Remember, the last time I saw you I told you I was working on a super-radio? This is it, a telepathy radio. I have succeeded in trapping those elusive emanations–thought-waves. I won't bore you with any explanation of the inner workings of the machine, It is enough that I went to the radio and the seismograph to produce it. I called you so that I could give you a demonstration, as I promised. You are the first person to whom I have shown it. Of course, I have given it a number of tests. It seems to be a success."

His eyes had lighted with ardor, and his voice had risen to an unusual pitch. But almost simultaneously this enthusiasm waned, and his face became very grave.

"You know, Brant," he said slowly. "I have never given up hope of finding Tom. I believe he is still living. I am sure of it. I want to find him. That was the incentive for this invention. I can locate him with this apparatus. That is what I am going to try to do tonight. If he lives, his mind will speak through this loud speaker. You understand the radio. Well, this machine is similar. It must be tuned into the thought-wave length of the man you wish to reach. But the machine must broadcast to receive, that is, the tuning ing[sic] consists of the broadcasting of a key thought. If you were seeking a murderer: you would broadcast some thought concerning the crime, whereupon the receiving section of the machine would draw in every unspoken reflection on it, and convert each into words. If your key thought were something known to many, perhaps published in the papers, the machine would utter a jumble of tones and voices, blurred by one another. It would be a Babel, so many thoughts, each from a different head. But then the operator would continue his broadcasting, thinking into the machine, With these pseudo-receiving phones, varying reflections on the crime, gradually leading to some clue, some phase known only to the police and the criminal. The million voices would instantly dwindle to a dozen or so, whereupon it would be easy to vary the wave-length a millionth part of a hairsbreadth, and so bring in the felon's thoughts, alone and clear. You may see then that I have a very dangerous contraption here, the more so since the mind is unaware that it is being tapped. I could accomplish great evil or great good with it. (But, as I said before, I made it only that I might find Tom, and now I shall make the attempt. There is a key thought that only he can respond to, an of our boyhood known, I believe, only to us.

He seated himself at the apparatus and adjusted the head-phones. He became intent, lasing into a deep study. I sat silent, tense with curiosity and awe, There was a long stillness,broken only by the ticking of the hall clock. The methodical sound of its mechanism so frayed my nerves that

I got up and stopped it. Then I tiptoed back to my seat. Dr. Spaulding had not noticed my move.

Presently, with an abruptness that made me start, the loudspeaker began to utter sounds. The doctor removed his headpiece and we leaned forward tautly. The sounds were unintelligible at first, then they became clear.

"It's Tom," murmurd[sic] the doctor, as he recognized the voice, and he looked happy for the first time in years.

"Dawn is coming," said the machine. "The first hint of light. Oh, God!"

There came a confusion of sounds, a jumble of incoherent words, then clearly:

"Here they come. I see the guards and the priest. Oh God! They are coming! They are coming!

"They walk so slowly, so solemnly. The guards and the priest. He is in his robe. I see his crucifix. It is swaying on its chain as he walks. The heels are beating so regularly. So perfectly in time. Oh God! The guards. They look grim, grim as the law! Law! It is law! There is no escape. Can I beat them down? The window. The door. A gun. Rush them when they open the door. They'll kill me. Kill me! The chair!

The doctor's face had gone white and drawn. He seemed turned to stone. His fingers were tight. The machine went on in its monotonous monotone.

"A rat is watching. Its eyes are bright. It is a gray rat. How long its nose is. Long and sharp. It is laughing. There. The key is turning. How slowly it grits. The bolt is drawn. The door is opening. It is opening slowly, so slowly. How gray everything is. How strange they look. The chair! There is no chance. Is there a chance? A chance? They are in … in a group. The guards have many buttons, one, two, three. The priest: how deep his eyes are. His face is very grave. He is talking. The rat is watching. Its eyes are bright, so bright. God save me!"

The sounds became incoherent and jangling. The doctor had not moved. The voice became audible again:

Now, walk, walk, walk. Click, click, click. Guards, so grim. I'll run. Useless. There's so much steel. Steel everywhere. I'm caught. I'm caught in the steel. The chair! Death! What will it be? Will it hurt? I must be quiet. I must not tremble. I must be brave. Walk, walk, walk. Now the little door. We are gong through. The chamber. How gray it is. Who are these men? There is a crowd. They are grim and sober. Some are white, and trembling. I am trembling. I must be brave. I must smile. But I am going to die! How silent it is. Oh God!

They are strapping me into the chair. I am putty. They are strapping me in. It is cold – so cold. I must be brave. I must smile and joke. But I am going to die. How still it is. They ave strapped me in. He has his hand on a lever. He is waiting to kill me. The current is going to be shot. God save me! It is cold. It is so dim. His hand is moving the lever--

"Oh Christ! Christ! I am bruised. I am burning. I am burning up. Oh God! ... Now I am numb. My flesh is sizzling and burning. I can feel it. I am writhing in the chair. But it doesn't hurt now. I can't move. My muscles won't move. I can't close my eyes. My mouth is dropped open. My jaws won't move. Am I paralized? Am—am I ... dead? Dead? No. Everything is the same. I can't be dead. The doctor is examining me. He says, 'I pronounce this man dead.'"

There was a pause. The doctor had not moved a muscle. His face was the hue of the grave. His eyes were indescribable, frozen.

He had not seized the significance of the last words, apparently, but I had. In spite of the horror I was sunk in, I realized that a theory of Dr. Spaulding's had been proven.

It was fully ten years since the doctor had aroused much interest with his attack on the use of the electric chair. It was his theory that in no case did electricity actually kill—that it merely brought on a paresis that simulated death, striking dormant the entire organism. He had cited instances of men struck by lightning, who had recovered, after many days, of total paralysis during which they retained only sight, hearing, and consciousness. Strange it was, and hideous, that tonight the doctor's own brother was proving the theory. The machine spoke again:

"The fool. He says I am dead. The fool. I wish I could talk. I would call him a fool. I would laugh at him. But I can't move.

"The men are leaving. The guards are unstrapping me. They catch me as I fall. Tehy are taking me out, through the little door. They are taking me down a long hall.

"I would like to shout at them. They think I am dead.

"The numbness has gone. I can feel their hands holding me. I can feel more intensely than before.

"They are carrying me into a room. What are they going to do? My God, are they going to bury me? No, it is the prison hospital. They are going to bring me to life. Thank the good God! They lay me on a table, the guards. But are they the guards? They act differently. Never mind.

"Ah, the surgeon is preparing to bring me to life. He is getting some instruments. He has a chisel or a saw or something in his hand. He is leaning above—

"Oh Christ! Oh bleeding Jesus! He is cutting my head—"

There sounded a wild scream. Dr. Spaulding leaped upon the machine, gibbering incoherently, and smashed the mechanism into a thousand pieces.

THROUGH the CRATER'S RIM

By A. Hyatt Verrill

But even as I gazed, transfixed with horror, paralyzed by the sight, the vine threw its last coil about the dying man and before my eyes drew the quivering body into the tree above. Then something approached my leg. With a wild yell of horror I leaped aside. A second vine was writhing and twisting over the ground towards me.

Introduction

In this story the author of "Beyond the Pole" gives us another one of his amasing contributions to Scientifiction. Here we find a strange race living within an extinct volcanic crater somewhere in Central America. When it is remembered that only a few years ago an entirely new race was discovered by scientists in Panama, which are now known better under the name of White Indians, it should be understood that Mr. Verrill is not taxing your credulity by the strange race which he pictures in this story.

We promise you a good half-hour's reading in this well-told tale.

THROUGH THE CRATER'S RIM

By A. Hyatt Verrill

CHAPTER I
Into the Unknown

I tell you it's there," declared Lieutenant Hazen decisively. "It may not be a civilized city, but it's no Indian village or native town. It's big—at least a thousand houses—and they're built of stone or something like it and not of thatch."

"You've been dreaming, Hazen," laughed Fenton. "Or else you're just trying to jolly us."

"Do you think I'd hand in an official report of a dream?" retorted the Lieutenant testily. "And it's gospel truth I've been telling you."

"Never mind Fenton," I put in. "He's a born pessimist and

skeptic anyhow. How much did you actually see?"

We were seated on the veranda of the Hotel Washington in Colon and the aviator had been relating how, while making a reconnaissance flight over the unexplored and unknown jungles of Darien, he had sighted an isolated, flat topped mountain upon whose summit was a large city—of a thousand houses or more—and without visible pass, road or stream leading to it.

"It was rotten air," Hazen explained in reply to my question. "And I couldn't get lower than 5,000 feet. So I can't say what the people were like. But I could see 'em running about the first time I went over and they were looking mightily excited. Then I flew back for a second look and not a soul was in sight—took to cover I expect. But I'll swear the buildings were stone or 'dobe and not palm or thatch."

"Why didn't you land and get acquainted?" enquired Fenton sarcastically.

"There was one spot that looked like a pretty fair landing," replied the aviator. "But the air was bad and the risk too big. How did I know the people weren't hostile? It was right in the Kuna Indian country and even if they were peaceable they might have smashed the plane or I mightn't have been able to take off. I was alone too."

"You say you made an official report of your discovery," I said. "What did the Colonel think about it?"

"Snorted and said he didn't see why in blazes I bothered reporting an Indian village."

"It's mighty interesting," I declared. "I believe you've actually seen the Lost City, Hazen. Balboa heard of it. The Dons spent years hunting for it and every Indian in Darien swears it exists."

"Well, I never heard of it before," said Hazen, "What's the

yarn, anyway?"

"According to the Indian story there's a big city on a mountain top somewhere in Darien. They say no one has ever visited it, that it's guarded by evil spirits and that it was there ages before the first Indians."

"If they've never seen it how do they know it's there?" Fenton demanded. "In my opinion it's all bosh. How can there be a 'lost city' in this bally little country and why hasn't someone found it? Why, there are stories of lost cities and hidden cities and such rot in every South and Central American country. Just fairy tales-pure bunk!"

"I know there are lots of such yarns," I admitted. "And most of them I believe are founded on fact. Your South American Indian hasn't enough imagination to make a story out of whole cloth. It's easy to understand why and how such a place might exist for centuries and no one find it. This 'little country' as you call it could hide a hundred cities in its jungles and no one be the wiser. No civilized man has ever yet been through the Kuna country. But I'm going. I'll have a try for that city of Hazen's."

"Well, I wish you luck," said Fenton. "If the Kunas don't slice off the soles of your feet and turn you loose in the bush and if you *do* find Hazen's pipe dream, just bring me back a souvenir, will you?"

With this parting shot he rose and sauntered off towards the swimming pool.

"Do you really mean to have a go at that place?" asked Hazen as Fenton disappeared.

"I surely do," I declared, "Can you show me the exact spot on the map where you saw the city?"

For the next half hour we pored over the map of Panama and while-owing to the incorrectness of the only available maps—Hazen could not be sure of the exact location of his discovery, still he pointed out a small area within which the strange city was located.

"You're starting on a mighty dangerous trip," he declared as I talked over my plans. "Even if you get by the Kunas and find the place how are you going to get out? The people may kill you or make you a prisoner. If they've been isolated for so long I reckon they won't let any news of 'em leak out."

"Of course there's a risk," I laughed. "That's what makes it so attractive. I'm not worried over the Kunas though. They're not half as bad as painted. I spent three weeks among them two years ago and had no trouble. They may drive me back, but they don't kill people offhand. Getting out will be the trouble as you say. But I've first got to get in and I'm not making plans to get out until then."

"Lord, but I wish I were going too!" cried Hazen. "Say, I tell you what I'm going to do. I'll borrow that old Curtiss practice boat and fly over there once in a while. If you're there, just wave a white rag for a signal. Maybe the people'll be so darned scared if they see the plane that they'll not trouble you. Might make a good play of it—let 'em think you're responsible for it you know."

"I don't know but that's mighty good scheme, Hazen," I replied, after a moment's thought. "Let's see. If I get off day after tomorrow I should be in the Kuna country in a week. You might take your first flight ten days from now. But if things go wrong I don't see as you can help me much if you can't land,"

"We'll worry over that when the time comes," he said cheerfully. A few days later I was being paddled and poled up the Canazas River with the last outposts of civilization many miles behind and the unknown jungles and the forbidden country of the wild Kunas ahead.

It was with the greatest difficulty that I had been able to secure men to accompany me, for the natives looked with the utmost dread upon the Kuna country and only two, out of the scores I had asked, were willing to tempt fate and risk their lives in the expedition into the unknown.

For two days now we had been within the forbidden district—the area guarded and held by the Kunas and into which no outsider is permitted to enter—and yet we had seen or heard no signs of Indians. But I was too old a hand and too familiar with the ways of South American Indians to delude myself with the idea that we had not been seen or our presence known. I well knew that, in every likelihood, we had been watched and our every movement known since the moment we entered the territory. No doubt, sharp black eyes were constantly peering at us from the jungle, while bows and blowguns were ever ready to discharge their missiles of death at any instant. As long as we were not molested or interfered with, however, I gave little heed to this. Moreover, I believed, from my brief acquaintance with the Kunas of two years previously, that they seldom killed a white man until after he had been warned out of their country and tried to return to it.

At night we camped beside the river, making our beds upon the warm dry sand and each day we poled the cayuca up the rapids and deeper into the forest. At last we reached the spot where, according to my calculations, we must strike through the jungle overland to reach the mountain seen by Hazen. Hiding our dugout in the thick brush beside the river we packed the few necessities to be carried with us and started off through the forest.

If Hazen were not mistaken in his calculations, we should

reach the vicinity of the mountain in two days' march, even though the going was hard and we were compelled to hew a way with our machetes for miles at a stretch.

But it's one thing to find a mountain top when flying over the sea of jungle and quite another to find that mountain when hidden deep in the forest and surrounded on every side by enormous trees. I realized that we might wander for days, searching for the mountain without finding it. It was largely a matter of luck after all. But Hazen had described the surrounding country so minutely, that I had high hopes of success.

By the end of the first day in the bush we had reached rough and hilly country, which promised well, and it was with the expectation of reaching the base of the mountain the following day that we made camp that night. Still we had seen no Indians, no signs of their trails or camps, which did much to calm the fears of my men and which I accounted for on the theory that the Kunas avoided this part of the country through superstitious fears of the lost city and its people.

At daybreak we broke camp and had tramped for perhaps three hours when, without warning, Jose, who was last in line, uttered a terrified cry. Turning quickly I was just in time to see him throw up his hands and fall in a heap with a long arrow quivering in his back. The Kunas were upon us.

Scarcely had the realization come to me when an arrow thudded sharply into a tree by my side and Carlos, with a wild yell of deadly fear, threw down his load and dashed madly away. Not an Indian could be seen. To stand there, a target for their missiles was suicidal, and turning, I fled at my utmost speed after Carlos. How we managed to run through that tangled jungle is still a mystery to me, but we made good time, nevertheless Fear drove us and dodging between the giant trees, leaping over rocks, we sped on.

And now, from behind, we could hear the sounds of the pursuing indians; their low guttural cries, the sounds of breaking twigs and branches; constantly they were drawing nearer. I knew that in a few minutes they would be upon us—that at any instant a poisoned blowgun dart or a barbed arrow might bury itself in my body; but still we strove to escape.

Then, just as I felt that the end must be at hand—just as I had decided to turn and sell my life dearly —the forest thinned. Before us sunlight appeared and the next moment we dashed from the jungle into a space free from underbrush but covered with enormous trees draped with gnarled and twisted lianas. The land here rose sharply and, glancing ahead between the trees, I saw the indistinct outlines of a lofty mountain against the sky.

Toiling up the slope, breathing heavily, utterly exhausted, I kept on. Then, as a loud shout sounded from the rear, I turned to see five hideously painted Kunas break from the jungle. But they did not follow. To my utter amazement they halted, gave a quick glance about, and, with a chorus of frightened yells, turned and dashed back into the shelter of the jungle.

But I had scant time to give heed to this. The Kunas' cries were still ringing in my ears when a scream from Carlos drew my attention. Thinking him attacked by savages I rushed toward him, drawing my revolver as I ran.

With bulging, rolling eyes, blanched face and ghastly, terror stricken features he was struggling, fighting madly, with a writhing, coiling gray object which I took for a gigantic snake. Already his body and legs were bound and helpless in the coils. With his machete he was raining blows upon the quivering awful thing which slowly, menacingly wavered back and forth before him, striving to throw another coil about his body.

And then as I drew near, my senses reeled, I felt that I was in some awful nightmare. The object, so surely, relentlessly, silently encircling and crushing him was no serpent but a huge liana drooping from the lofty branches of a great tree!

It seemed absolutely incredible, impossible, unbelievable. But even as I gazed, transfixed with horror, paralyzed by the sight, the vine threw its last coil about the dying man and before my eyes drew the quivering body into the trees above.

Then something touched my leg. With a wild yell of terror I leaped aside. A second vine was writhing and twisting over the ground towards me! Crazed with unspeakable fear I struck at the thing with my machete. At the blow the vine drew sharply back while from the gash a thick, yellowish, stinking juice oozed forth. Turning, I started to rush from the accursed spot but as I passed the first tree another liana writhed forward in my path.

Utterly bereft of my senses, slashing madly as I ran, yelling like a madman, 1 dodged from tree to tree, seeking the open spaces, evading by a hair's breadth the fearful, menacing, serpent-like vines, until half-crazy, torn, panting and utterly spent dashed forth into a clear grassy space. Before me, rising like a sheer wall against the sky was a huge precipitous cliff of red rock. Now I knew why the Kunas had not followed us beyond the jungle. They were aware of the man-killing lianas and had left us to a worse death than any they could inflict. I was safe from them I felt sure. But was I any better off? Before me was an impassable mountain side. On either hand and in the rear those awful, bloodthirsty, sinister vines and, lurking in the jungles, were the savage Kunas with their fatal poisoned darts and powerful bows. I was beset on every side by deadly peril, for I was without food, I had cast aside my gun and even my revolver in my blind, terror-crazed escape from those ghastly living vines, and to remain where I was meant death by starvation or thirst.

But anything was better than this nightmare-like forest. At the thought I glanced with a shudder at the trees and my blood seemed to freeze in my veins.

The forest was approaching me? I could not believe my eyes. Now I felt I must be mad, and fascinated, hypnotized, I gazed, striving my utmost to clear my brain, to make common sense contradict the evidence of my eyes. But it was no delusion. Ponderously, slowly, but steadily the trees were gliding noiselessly up the slope! Their great gnarled roots were creeping and undulating over the ground while the pendant vines writhed and swayed and darted forth in all directions as if feeling their way. And then I saw what had before escaped me. The things were not lianas as I thought—huge, lithe, flexible tentacles springing from a thick, fleshy livid-hued crown of branches armed with stupendous thorns and which slowly opened and closed like hungry jaws above the huge trunks.

It was monstrous, uncanny, supernatural. A hundred yards and more of open ground had stretched between me and the forest when I had flung myself down, but now a scant fifty paces remained. In a few brief moments the fearsome things would be upon me. But I was petrified, incapable of moving hand or foot, too terrified and overwhelmed even to cry out.

Nearer and nearer the ghastly things came. I could hear the pounding of my heart. A cold sweat broke out on my body. I shivered as with ague. Then a long, warty, tentacle darted towards me and as the loathsome stinking thing touched my hand the spell was broken. With a wild scream I turned and dashed blindly towards the precipice, seeking only to delay, only to avoid for a time the certain awful death to which I was doomed, for the cliff barred all escape and I could go no further.

CHAPTER II
Amazing Discoveries

A dozen leaps and I reached the wall of rock beyond which all retreat was cut off. Close at hand was an outjutting buttress, and thinking that back of this I might hide and thus prolong my life, I raced for it.

Panting, unseeing, I reached the projection, ducked behind it, and to my amazement and unspeakable delight, found myself in a narrow canyon or defile, like a huge cleft in the face of the precipice.

Here was safety for a time. The terrible man-eating trees could not enter, and striving only to put a greater distance between myself and the vegetable demons I never slackened my pace as I turned and sped up the canyon.

Narrower and narrower it became. Far above my head the rocky walls leaned inward, shutting out the light until soon it was so dim and shadowy that, through sheer necessity, I was forced to stop running and to pick my way carefully over the masses of rock that strewed the canyon's floor. Presently only a narrow ribbon of sky was visible between the towering walls of the pass. Then this was blotted out and I found myself in the inky blackness of a tunnel—an ancient watercourse—leading into the very bowels of the mountain.

But there was no use in hesitating. Anything was preferable to the cannibal trees, and groping my way I pressed on. Winding and twisting, turning sharply, the passageway led, ever ascending steeply and taxing my exhausted muscles and overwrought system to the utmost. Then, far ahead, I heard the faint sound of dripping, falling water and with joy at thought of burying my aching head in the cold liquid, and of easing my parched, dry throat, I hurried, stumbling, through the tunnel.

At last, I saw a glimmer of light in the distance and in it the sparkle of the water. Before me was the end of the tunnel and sunlight and with a final spurt of speed I rushed towards it. Then, just as I gained the opening, and so suddenly and unexpectedly that he seemed to materialize from thin air, a man rose before me.

Unable to check my speed, too thunderstruck at the apparition to halt. I dashed full into him and together we rolled head over heels upon the ground,

I have said he was a man. But even in that brief second that I glimpsed him, before I bowled him over, I realized that he was unlike any man I or anyone else had ever seen. Barely three feet in height, squat, with enormous head and shoulders, he stood shakily upon the tiniest of bandy legs and half supported his weight by his enormously long muscular arms. Had it not been that he was partly clothed and that his face was hairless, I should have thought him an ape. And now, as I picked myself up and stared at him, my jaws gaped in utter amazement. The fellow was running from me at top speed upon his hands, his feet waving and swaying in the air!

So utterly dumbfounded was I at the sight that I stood there silently gazing after the strange being until he vanished behind a clump of bushes. Then as it dawned upon me that as he had shown no sign of hostility, they were likely peaceable, I hurried after him.

A narrow trail led through the brush and running along

this I burst from the shrubbery and came to an abrupt halt, utterly astounded at the sight which met my eyes. I was standing at the verge of a little rise beyond which stretched an almost circular, level plain several miles in diameter. Massed upon this in long rows, compact groups and huge squares, were hundreds of low, flat-roofed, stone buildings, while upon a smooth green plot at a little distance, stood a massive truncated pyramid.

Unwittingly I had reached my goal.

Before me was the lost city of Darien. Hazen had been right!

But it was not this thought not the strange city and its buildings that held my fascinated gaze, but the people. Everywhere they swarmed. Upon the streets, the housetops, even on the open land of the plain, they crowded and each and every one an exact counterpart of the one with whom 1 had collided at the mouth of the tunnel. And, like him too, all were walking or running upon their hands with their feet in air!

All this I saw in the space of a few seconds. Then, to add to my astonishment, I saw that many of the impossible beings actually were carrying burdens in their upraised feet! Some bore baskets, others jars or pots, others bundles, while one group that was approaching in my direction, held bows and arrows in their toes, and held them most menacingly at that!

It was evident that I had been seen. The excitement of the beings, their gestures and the manner in which they peered toward me from between their arms, left no doubt of it, while the threatening defensive attitude of the bowmen proved that they were ready to attack or defend at a moment's notice.

No doubt, to them, my appearance was as remarkable, as inexplicable and as amazing as they were to me. The greater portion were evidently filled with terror and scurried into their houses, yet many still stood their ground, while a few were so overcome with curiosity and surprise that they dropped feet to earth and rested right side up in order to stare at me more intently.

I realized that it behooved me to do something. To stand there motionless and speechless, gazing at the strange folk while they stared back, would accomplish nothing. But what to do, what move to make? That was a serious question. If I attempted to approach them a shower of arrows might well end my career and my investigations of the place then and there. It was equally useless to retrace my steps, even had I been so minded, for only certain death lay back of me. By some means I must win the confidence or friendship of these outlandish beings if only temporarily. A thousand ideas flashed through my mind.

If only Hazan would appear the creatures of the city might think I had dropped from the sky and so look upon me as a supernatural being. But it was hopeless to expect such a coincidence or to look for him. I had told him to fly over on the tenth day and this was only the seventh. If only I had retained my revolver the discharge of the weapon might frighten them into thinking me a god. But my firearms lay somewhere in the demon forest, I had heard no sounds of voices, no shouting, and I wondered if the beings were dumb. Maybe, I thought, if I should speak—should yell—I might impress them. But, on the other hand, the sound of my voice might break the spell and cause them to attack me. A single mistake, the slightest false move, might seal my doom. I was in a terrible quandary. All my former experiences with savage unknown tribes passed through my mind, and I strove to think of some incident, some little event, which had saved the day in the past and might be put to good use now.

And as I thus pondered I unconsciously reached in my pocket for my pipe, filled it with tobacco and placing it between my lips, struck a match and puffed forth a cloud of smoke. Instantly, from the weird-creatures, a low, wailing, sibilant sound arose. The archers dropped their bows and arrows and, with one accord, the people threw themselves grovelling on the ground. Unintentionally I had solved the problem. To these beings I was a fire-breathing, awful god!

Realizing this, knowing that when dealing with primitive races full of superstitions one must instantly follow up an advantage, I hesitated no longer. Puffing lustily at my pipe I strode forward and approached the nearest prostrate group. Motionless they buried their faces in the dust, bodies pressed to earth, not daring to look up or even steal a surreptitious glance at the terrible, smoke-belching being who towered over them. Never had I seen such a demonstration of abject fear, such utter debasement. It really was pitiful to see them, to view their trembling, panting bodies quivering with nameless terror; terror so great they dared not flee, even though they knew by my footsteps that I was among them, and feared that at any moment an awful doom might descend upon them.

But their very fright defeated my purpose. I had won safety and even adoration perhaps, but there could be no amity, no intercourse, no means of mingling with them, of securing food, of learning anything if they were to remain cowering on the ground. By some means I must win a measure of their confidence, I must prove that I was a friendly beneficent deity and yet I must still be able to impress them with my powers and control through fear.

It was a delicate matter to accomplish, but it had to be done. Almost at my feet lay one of the archers — a leader or chieftain I thought from the feather ornaments he wore—and stooping, I lifted, him gently. At my touch he fairly palpitated with terror, but no frightened scream, no sound save an indrawn snake-like hiss, escaped his lips, and he offered no resistance as I lifted him to a kneeling position.

Hitherto I had had no opportunity to obtain a good view of these people, but now I saw this fellow close at hand I was amazed at his repulsive ugliness. I have seen some rather ugly races, but all of them combined and multiplied a hundredfold would be beauties compared to these dwarfed, topsy-turvy, denizens of the lost city. Almost black, low browed, with tiny, shifty eyes like those of a reptile, with enormous, thick lipped mouths, sharp, fang-like teeth and matted hair, the bowman seemed far more like an ape than like a human being. And then I noticed a most curious thing. He had no ears! Where they should have been were merely round, bare spots covered with light colored thin membrane like the ears of a frog. For an instant I thought it a malformation or an injury. But as I glanced at the others I saw that all were the same. Not one possessed a human ear! All this I took in as I lifted the fellow up. Then as he tremblingly raised his head and eyed me I spoke to him, trying to make my tones gentle and reassuring. But there was no response, no sign of intelligence or understanding in his dull, frightened eyes. There was nothing to do but to fall back on sign language and rapidly I gestured, striving to convey to him that I would do no injury or harm, that I was friendly and that I wished the people to rise. Slowly a look of comprehension dawned upon his ugly face and then, to prove my friendship, I fished in my pocket, found a tiny mirror and placed it in his hand. At the expression of utter astonishment that overspread his ugly features as he looked in the glass I roared with laughter. But the mirror won the day. Uttering sharp, strange, hissing sounds, the fellow conveyed the news to his companions and slowly, hesitatingly and with lingering fear still on their faces, the people rose and gazed upon me with strangely mingled awe and curiosity.

Mainly they were men, but scattered among them were many who evidently were women, although all were so uniformly repulsive in features that it was difficult to distinguish the sexes. All too, were clad much alike in single garments of bark-cloth resembling gunny sacks with, holes cut at the four corners for legs and arms and an opening for the head.

But while there was no variation in the form or material of the clothing yet some wore ornaments and others did not. Leg and arm bands of woven fibre were common. Many of the men had decorations of bright hued feathers attached to arms or legs or fastened about their waists and many were elaborately tattooed. That such primitive dwarfed, ugly, degenerate creatures could have built the city of stone houses, could have laid out the broad paved streets and could have developed so much of civilization, seemed incredible.

But I had little time to devote to such thoughts. The fellow I had presented with the mirror was hissing at me like a serpent and by signs was trying to indicate that I was to follow him. So, with the crowd trailing behind us, we started up the road towards the centre of the city.

CHAPTER III
Before the King

Truly no stranger procession had ever been seen by human eyes.

Before me, the chief archer led the way, walking upon his great calloused hands and with his bow grasped firmly in one prehensile foot and his precious mirror in the other. On either side and in the rear were scores of the weird beings hurrying along on their hands, keeping up an incessant hissing sound like escaping steam; black legs and feet waving and gesticulating in air and, at first glance, appearing like a crowd of headless dwarfs. How I wished that Fenton might have been there to see!

Apparently my actions had been closely watched from the safe retreats of the houses and word passed that I was not to be feared, for as we reached the first buildings, the edges of the roofs and the tiny window slits were lined with curious, ugly faces peering at us. It was then that I noticed that none of the buildings had doors, the walls rising blank to the roofs save for the narrow windows, while ladders, here and there in place, proved that the inhabitants, like the Pueblo Indians, entered and left their dwellings through the roofs.

Now and then as we passed along, some of the more venturesome beings would join the procession, scrambling nimbly down the ladders, sometimes upside down on their hands, often using both hands and feet, but always using hands only as soon as they reached the ground.

How or why they had developed this extraordinary mode of progression puzzled me greatly, for there seemed no scientifically good reason for it. Among tribes who habitually use boats, weak legs and enormously developed shoulders, chests and arms are common, and I could well understand how a race, depending entirely upon water for transportation, might, through generations of inbreeding and isolation, lose the use of legs.

But here was a people who apparently had no conveyances of any kind, who must of necessity travel about to cultivate their crops, who must carry heavy burdens in order to construct their buildings and to whom legs would seem a most important matter, and yet with legs and feet so atrophied and arms so tremendously developed that they walked on their hands and used their feet as auxiliaries. It was a puzzle I longed to solve and that I would have investigated thoroughly had fate permitted me to dwell longer in the strange city. But I am getting ahead of my story.

Presently we reached a large central square surrounded by closely set buildings. Approaching one of these, my guide signalled that I was to follow him as he swiftly ascended the ladder to the roof. Rather hesitatingly, for I doubted if the frail affair would support my weight, I climbed gingerly up and found myself upon the broad, flat roof. Before me were several dark openings with the ends of ladders projecting from them and down one of these my guide led the way. At the bottom of the ladder I was in a large, obscure room, lit only by the slits of windows high in the walls, and for a moment I could see nothing of my surroundings, although from all sides issued the low hissing sounds that I now knew were the language of these remarkable people. Then, as my eyes became accustomed to the dim light, I saw that a score of beings were squatted about the sides of the room, while, directly before me, on a raised dais or platform, was seated the largest and ugliest individual I had seen.

That he was a ruler, a king or high priest, was evident. In place of the sack-like garment of his people he was clad in a long rove of golden green feathers. Upon his head was a feather crown of the same hue. About his wrists and ankles were golden bands studded with huge uncut emeralds, and a string of the same stones hung upon his chest.

The throne, if such it could be called, was draped with a green and gold rug and everywhere, upon the walls of the chamber, were paintings of strange misshapen, uncouth creatures and human beings all in the same green and yellow tints. Something in the surroundings, in the drawings and the costume of the king, reminded me of the Aztecs or Mayas and while quite distinct from either I felt sure that, in some long past time, these dwellers of the lost city had been influenced by or had been in contact with, these ancient civilizations.

As I stood before the dais my guide prostrated himself before the green robed monarch and then rising, carried on what appeared to be an animated account of my arrival and the subsequent happenings.

As he spoke, silence fell upon those present and the king listened attentively, glancing now and then at me and regarding me with an expression of combined fear, respect and enmity. I could readily understand what his feelings were. No doubt he was a person of far greater intelligence than his subjects, and while more or less afraid of such a strange being as myself, and superstitious enough to think me supernatural, yet in me he saw a possible usurper of his own power and prominence and, if he had dared, he would have been only too glad to have put me out of the way.

At the end of the archer's narrative the fellow handed his mirror to the king who uttered a sharp exclamatory hiss as he saw his own ugly countenance reflected in it. Forgetting court etiquette and conventions in their curiosity, the others gathered about and as the mirror passed from hand to hand their amazement knew no bounds.

All of these men I now saw were clad in green or green and white and were evidently of high rank, priests or courtiers I took it, but otherwise were as undersized and repulsive as the common people on the streets.

Suddenly I was aroused from my contemplation of the

room and its occupants by my guide who came close and by signs ordered me to perform the miracle of smoking. Very ceremoniously and deliberately I drew out my pipe, filled it and struck a match. At the bright flare of the flame king and courtiers uttered a wailing hiss of fear and threw themselves upon the floor. But they were of different stuff from their people, or else the guide had prepared them for the event, for the king soon raised his head, and glancing dubiously at me and finding I had not vanished in fire and smoke, as he no doubt expected, he resumed his sitting posture and in sharp tones ordered his fellows to do likewise.

But despite this it was very evident that he and his friends were in dread of the smoke from my mouth and nose while the tobacco fumes caused them to sputter and cough and choke. This at last was more than even the king could stand, and by signs he made it clear that he wished me to end the demonstration of my fire eating ability. Then he rose, and, to my unbounded surprise, stood erect and stepped forward like an ordinary mortal upon his feet. Here was an extraordinary thing. Was the king of a distinct race or stock or was the use of nether limbs for walking confined to the royal family or to individuals?

It was a fascinating scientific problem to solve. I had no time to give it any consideration, however, for the king was now addressing me in his snake-like dialect and was trying hard to make his meaning clear by signs. For a moment I was at a loss, but presently I grasped his meaning. He was asking whence I had come, and from the frequency with which he pointed upward I judged he thought I had dropped from the sky.

Then a brilliant idea occurred to me as I remembered Hazan's story and his suggestion regarding his return by plane. Pointing upward I made the best imitation of a motor's exhaust that I could manage. There was no doubt that the monarch grasped the meaning. He grinned, nodded and swept his arm in a wide semicircle around his head, evidently to represent the course of the plane when Hazen had flown over the city.

Seemingly, satisfied and, I judged, deeply impressed as well, he resumed his seat, gave a few orders to his fellows and summoning my guide spoke a few words to him. Thereupon the archer signalled me to follow and led the way across the room. But I noticed that the king had not returned the mirror.

Ascending the ladder to the roof the fellow hurried across to a second building, scrambled down another ladder and we entered a large room. In one corner swung a large fiber hammock; in the centre was spread cloth decorated in green and gold, and as we entered two women appeared, each carrying handsome earthenware dishes of food whose savory odors whetted my already ravenous appetite.

Marvelous as it was to see these impossible beings carrying food in their uplifted feet and walking on their hands, yet I had now become somewhat accustomed to the people and I was so famished that I hardly gave the upside down serving maids a second glance.

The food was excellent—consisting of vegetables, some sort of fricassee game and luscious fruits—and as I ate my guide squatted near and regarded me with the fixed, half adoring, half frightened look that one sees on the face of a strange puppy.

I judged that he had been appointed my own personal guard or valet—it mattered little which—and I was not sorry, for he seemed a fairly decent specimen of his race and we already had become pretty well accustomed to each other's signs and gestures. Wishing to still further establish myself in his confidence, and feeling rather sorry for him because of the loss of his treasured mirror, I searched my pockets for some other trinket. My possessions however were limited. They consisted of a stub of a lead-pencil, a note book, a few coins, my handkerchief, my watch, my pocket-knife, a few loose pistol cartridges, my pipe and tobacco and a box of matches. As I drew all these out a sudden fear gripped me. I had barely a dozen matches remaining and my supply of tobacco was perilously low, What would happen when I could no longer produce fire and smoke when called upon to do so?

But I controlled my fears and comforted myself with the thought that possibly, after having felt the effects of tobacco smoke, the king would not soon demand another miracle at my hands and that, before either matches or tobacco was exhausted, something might well happen to solve any problems that might arise. Nevertheless I heartily wished that I had arranged with Hazen to bring supplies in case they were needed and which he could have easily dropped as he flew over.

It would, I now realized, have proved an extremely impressive thing for the people to have seen me secure my magic from the giant roaring bird in the sky. But I had never of course dreamed of such adventures as I had met and could not possibly have foreseen the need of such things. Just the same I cursed myself for a stupid fool for not having provided for any contingency and especially for not having arranged a series of signals with Hazen, However, I was familiar with wigwagging and decided that, if necessity arose, it would be quite feasible for me to signal to him by means of my handkerchief tied on a stick. Also, I felt a bit easier in my mind from knowing that near the city was a splendid landing place for the plane and that Hazen, if signalled, would unquestionably attempt a descent.

Truly it was not every explorer in a predicament like mine who could count on being able to summon aid from the clouds if worst came to worst or who knew that a friend in an airplane would keep track of his whereabouts, indeed, I almost chuckled at these incredible folk and yet within two hundred miles of the Canal and civilization and with another American due to hover above—and even communicate with me—within the next three days. It was all so dreamlike, so utterly preposterous that I scarcely could force myself to believe it and, having dined well and feeling desperately tired, I flung myself into the hammock and almost instantly dropped off to sleep.

It was still daylight when I awoke and the room was empty. Ascending the ladder to the roof without meeting anyone, I climbed down the other ladder to the street. Many people were about and while a few, especially the women and children, threw themselves on their faces or scampered into their houses at my approach, yet the majority merely prostrated themselves for a moment and then stood, supporting themselves in their ape-like way, and stared curiously at me. I had gone but a short distance when my valet came hurrying to my side. But he made no objections to my going where I wished and I was glad to see that my movements were not to be hampered as I was anxious thoroughly to explore the city and its neighborhood. Curious to learn the purpose of the pyramidal structure I had noticed I proceeded in that direction and was soon in a part of the town given over to stalls, shops and markets. There were also several workshops, such as pottery makers', a woodworking shop and a weaver's shop and I spent some time watching the artisans at their work. Somehow, from seeing the people walk upon their hands, I had expected to see them perform their tasks with their feet and it came as something of a surprise to see these fellows using their hands like ordinary mortals.

Beyond this portion of the city the houses were scattered, the outlying buildings were more or less patched and out of repair and were very evidently the abode of the poorer classes, although the inhabitants I saw, and who retreated the instant they saw me, were exactly like all the others as far as I could see, both in dress and feature. Passing these huts, I crossed the smooth green field, which I now saw was a perfect landing place for the plane. Tethered to stakes and grazing on the grass were a number of animals which, as I first noticed them, I had taken for goats and cattle. But now I discovered that they were all deer and tapirs. It was a great surprise to see these animals domesticated but, after all, it was not remarkable, for I should have known, had I stopped to give the matter thought, that goats, sheep and cattle were unknown to the aboriginal Americans and that this city and its people, who had never been visited and had never communicated with other races, would of necessity be without these well known animals.

Moreover, I knew that the Mayas were supposed to have used tapirs as beasts of burden, and while I was standing there watching the creatures a man approached riding astride a big tapir and driving a second one loaded with bags of charcoal and garden produce. Here then was a partial solution of the manner by which these weak, dwarfed people built their stone houses. For with the powerful elephant-like tapirs—and I noticed all were the giant Baird's tapir which reaches a weight of seven or eight hundred pounds—they could easily haul the blocks of stone from a quarry and by means of tackle and inclined planes, could readily hoist the stones to the tops of the walls.

I had now reached the base of the pyramid and found it a massive structure of the same flinty stone as the other buildings. Running from base to summit was a spiral path or stairway and instantly I knew that it was a sacrificial pyramid exactly like those used by the Aztecs and on which unfortunate beings were killed and sacrificed. This discovery still further confirmed my suspicions that these people were either of Aztec or Maya blood or had been influenced by those races. Filled with curiosity to see the altar on the summit I started up the sloping stairs. I was at first doubtful if my companion would permit this for the structure was sacred and doubtless only priests of the highest order were permitted upon it. Evidently, however, my guide thought that such a supernatural being or god as myself had every right to invade the most sacred places, and he offered no objection, but prostrated himself at the base of the pyramid as I ascended. At the summit I found, as I had expected, the sacrificial stone, a huge block elaborately carved in hieroglyphs and with channels to permit the blood to drain off, while, close at hand, was a massive carved stone collar or yoke exactly like those which have been found in Puerto Rico and have so long puzzled scientists. From the blood stains upon this I felt sure it was used to hold down the victim's head and neck, while strong metal staples, set into the stone, indicated that the man destined for sacrifice was spread-eagled and his ankles and wrists bound fast to the rings.

It was a most interesting spot from a scientific standpoint, but decidedly gruesome, while the stench of putrefied blood and fragments of human flesh clinging to the stones was nauseating and I was glad to retrace my steps and descend to the ground.

From the top of the pyramid I had obtained a fine view of the plain and city and I had noted that the former was surrounded on all sides with steep cliffs, and I realized that the plain was not a flat topped mountain as I had thought but the crater of an extinct volcano.

I saw no path, pass or opening by which the crater-valley could be entered, but I knew there was the one by which I had arrived. As the sun, here on the mountain top, was still well above the horizon I decided to visit the entrance to the tunnel, for I was anxious to know what the people should leave this avenue open when, on every other side, they were completely cut off from the outer world. Possibly, I thought, they knew of those horrible man-eating trees and trusted to them to guard the city from intruders. Or again, they might keep the entrance guarded, for the fellow I had knocked over as I dashed in had been at the tunnel mouth and for all I knew he might have been an armed guard and was merely so thunderstruck at my precipitate appearance that he forgot his duties and his weapons.

With such thoughts running through my mind I strolled across the plain, past well-tilled gardens and fields, in several of which I saw men ploughing with well made plows drawn by tapirs. Even the farmers stopped their work and prostrated themselves as I passed, and it was evident that word of my celestial origin and supernatural character had gone forth to every inhabitant of the valley.

Following the path, I reached the little rise from which I had first viewed the city and soon came to the spot where I had entered. Imagine my utter surprise when I saw no sign whatever of the opening. I was positive that I had not missed my way. I recognized the clumps of bushes and the forms of the rocks, but there was no dark hole, no aperture in the cliff. Then, as I drew near to the precipice, I made an astounding discovery. Closely fitted into the rock and so like it that it had escaped my attention, was an enormous stone door. How it was operated, whether it was hinged or slid or whether it was pivoted, I could not determine. But that it covered and concealed the entrance to the tunnel I was convinced. Why the people had left the tunnel open as though to clear the way for me, why they should have fitted a door to it, why they should ever use the tunnel which could bring them only to the death-dealing forest, were problems which I could not solve.

At any rate there was nothing to be gained by staying there and I started back towards the city. Thinking to return by another route, I took a path that led towards the opposite mountain side and presently from ahead, I distinctly heard the sound of metal striking stone.

Oddly enough my mind had been so filled with other matters that I had hardly wondered how these people cut or worked the hard stone. But now that my attention was attracted by the sound my curiosity was aroused and I hurried forward. What metal I wondered, did these people use? For metal I knew it must be from the ringing, clinking noise. Was I about to see hardened bronze tools in actual use or had these marvelous folk discovered the use of iron or steel? So astounding had been all my experiences, so paradoxical and incredible everything I had seen, that I was prepared for almost anything. I, or rather we, soon came to the verge of a deep pit wherein, laboring at great masses of white stone, were scores of workmen. Standing like skeletons among the blocks were derricks; hitched to sledge-like drags loaded with stone were teams of tapirs and on the further side was a big outjutting. Hurrying down the steep trail I reached the bottom of the pit to find every man flat on the ground. Signalling to my companion that I wished to have the fellows go on with their work, I approached the nearest slab of rock. It was the same fine grained whitish rock of which the city was built, and, lying upon it where they had been dropped by the stone cutters, were several small hammers, chisels and an adze-like tool. That they were not bronze or any alloy of copper I knew at the first glance. Their color was that of tempered steel and they seemed ridiculously small for the purpose of working this hard stone. If these people used steel then I had indeed made a discovery, and intent on this matter I picked up one of the tools to examine it. No sooner had I lifted it that I uttered an involuntary exclamation of surprise. The hammer, although hardly larger than an ordinary tack hammer, weighed fully ten pounds! It was heavier than if made of solid gold. There was only one known metal that could be so heavy and that was platinum. But platinum it could not be, for that metal is softer than gold and would be of no more use for cutting rock than so much lead. The tools, however, were undoubtedly hard—the polished surface of the hammer-head and the chisels, and the unscarred keen edges of the latter, showed this, and, anxious to test their hardness, I held a chisel against the rock and struck it sharply with a hammer.

Once more I cried out in wonder, for the chisel had bitten fully half an inch into the stone! It had cut it as easily as if the rock were cheese! What marvel was this? What magic lay in these tools? And then the secret dawned upon me and a moment's examination of the stone confirmed my suspicions. It was not that the tools were so very hard or keen but that the rock was soft—so soft that I could readily cut it with my pocket knife, a wax-like earthy rock which no doubt became hard upon exposure to the air exactly like the coral rock of Bermuda, which may be quarried with saws and even planed, but becomes as hard as limestone after exposure to the elements. Still, the tools were far harder than any metal except tempered steel, and for some time I puzzled over the matter as I watched the workmen, now over their fright and adoration, skillfully cutting and squaring the blocks of stone. It was one more conundrum I could not solve, and it was not until long afterwards, when a careful analysis of the metal was made, that I knew the truth. The metal was an alloy of platinum and iridium—the later one of the hardest of all known metals.

As we left the quarry and made our way toward the city I noticed an immense aqueduct stretching across the land from the apparently solid mountain side just above the quarry. I had given little thought to how the people secured water here in the crater. But it was now apparent that it was brought from some source by the stone conduit. Keenly curious to know whence it came, for I could not imagine how a river, lake or spring could exist on the crater rim, I wished to investigate, but darkness was coming on, I was tired and I deferred further exploration until another day.

Although I suppose I should have been grateful for being able to communicate with the people at all, yet I keenly felt the lack of a common medium of conversation, for the sign language was limited and I could not secure information I so much desired about many matters that puzzled me.

Nothing further of interest transpired that night. I was supplied with food, I slept soundly and did not awaken until roused by the women with my breakfast. Very soon afterwards I was summoned to the throne room by Zip, as I called my companion, and once more I had to strike a match and smoke my pipe for the king's benefit. This time a second personage of high rank was beside him, a villainous looking hunchbacked dwarf with red, vicious eyes and cruel mouth but who, like the king, walked on his feet. From his elaborately decorated white robes and the mitre-like crown of quetzal feathers on his gray head, I concluded he was a high priest, for in the designs upon his costume and the form of his crown, I saw a decided resemblance to the Aztec priests as shown in the picturegraph of that race. Moreover, the quetzal or resplendant trogon was, I knew, the sacred bird of the Aztecs and Mayas, and while I was aware that it was common in the northern portions of Panama, I had never heard of its occurrence in Darien, a fact which still further confirmed in my belief that these people were of Aztec stock. But if this were the case it was a puzzle as to why they should be so undersized, malformed and physically degenerate, for both the Aztecs and Mayas were powerful, well-formed races. The only solution I could think of was the supposition that isolation and intermarriage through centuries had brought about such results.

But to return to my audience with the king. I was not all pleased at thus having to use my precious matches and tobacco and I foresaw some very unpleasant developments in store for me if the performance was to be of daily occurrence. It was manifest that I must devise some new and startling exhibition of my powers if I were to retain my prestige and my freedom, for I well knew, from past experiences with savage races, and from the character of these potentates, that if I failed to perform miracles, and became, in their eyes, an ordinary mortal, my career would come to an abrupt end.

To be sure, there was the reassuring fact that Hazen would or should appear within the nest forty-eight hours, but it was decidedly problematical as to whether I could communicate with him or could receive any aid from the air. However, there was nothing to be done but obey and puff away at my pipe. With the idea of cutting the exhibition short I stepped closer to the throne and blew the smoke towards the faces of the king and the priest. The monarch was soon coughing and spluttering, but he was game, while the priest, to my amazement, sniffed the smoke and seemed to enjoy it. Here was trouble. Evidently he had a natural taste for tobacco and this fact caused me a deal of worry, for if the old rascal took it into his head to acquire the habit and demanded I should let him try a puff at the pipe I would be in a pretty fix indeed.

However, my fears on this score were groundless, and presently the king, who could stand it no longer, signalled for me to depart, which I did most gladly.

I still had it in mind to investigate the water supply, and with Zip—reminding me of an acrobatic clown— beside me, headed for the aqueduct. This I found was of stones, dovetailed together in water tight joints, and built like an open trough and the speed of the water flowing though it proved the supply well above the city's level. It was an easy matter to follow the conduit, for a well-trodden path was beside it, but it was a steep upgrade climb for nearly a mile before I gained the spot where the aqueduct tapped the mountain rim. Here the water gushed from a hole in the solid rock and from its volume I knew it must come from some large reservoir. From where I stood I could look directly down into the quarry and the thought flashed through my mind that if the people continued to quarry in the place for many more years they would undermine and weaken the foundations of the aqueduct.

It was their lookout not mine, however, and still intent on tracing the water to its source I turned up a trail that appeared to lead to the mountain top. In places this was excessively steep and here Zip exhibited a new habit of his people. Dropping his feet first and his prehensile toes grasping every projection and bit of rock to draw him along while his immense, powerful hands supported his weight; and pushed him onward. He looked more like a gigantic spider than anything, and not in the least human. Panting and blown I at last gained the summit and looked down upon a lake of dismal black water filling a circular crater about half a mile in diameter. Close by was an aperture in the rock and half-filled with water, and it was evident that this was connected with the outlet below by means of a shaft. Whether this was a natural formation or had been laboriously cut by hand I could not tell, but I was prepared for almost anything by this time and was not greatly surprised to find a cleverly constructed sluice gate arranged above the opening to regulate the flow of water. I had seen similar crater lakes in the extinct volcanoes of the West Indies, but I was surprised that Hazen had not mentioned it. But on second thought I realized that when flying over it, the dark water surrounded by vegetation would hardly be visible and might easily be mistaken for heavy shadow or an empty crater, while the aviator's surprise at the city would fix his attention upon it to the exclusion of all surroundings.

Standing upon the rock ridge several hundred feet above the city I had almost the same view as Hazen had from his plane and I could understand how, at an elevation of 5000 feet or more, he had been unable to obtain any very accurate idea of the buildings or people. I also realized, with a sinking of my heart, that it would be next to impossible for him to recognize me or to see any signals I might make.

The most prominent spot in the entire valley was the pyramid, for this was isolated upon the green plain and the sun, striking through a gap in the eastern rim of the crater, shone directly upon the altar's summit, this bringing it out in sharp relief. Indeed, it looked for all the world like a pylon on an aviation field. If I expected to make my presence known to Hazen or to signal to him, my best point of vantage would be the summit of the pyramid and I determined to climb there and await his arrival when he should be due, two days later.

Little did I dream at the time of the conditions under which I would await him upon that gruesome altar.

CHAPTER IV
The Sacrifice

By the time we had descended the mountain and had reached the city it was noon, and going to my quarters I was glad to find an excellent meal. Having finished eating I threw myself into the hammock and despite my scarcity of matches and tobacco, indulged in a smoke. Then, feeling drowsy, I took off my coat, placed it on the floor beside my hammock and closed my eyes.

I awoke refreshed and reached for my coat only to leap from the hammock with a cry of alarm. The coat was gone! Quickly I searched the room, thinking Zip might have placed the garment elsewhere while I slept, but the place was bare. Zip was nowhere to be seen, and even the rug on which meals were served had been removed.

Here was a pretty state of affairs. My coat contained my matches, pipe, tobacco, pocket knife and handkerchief.

Without it I was lost, helpless, incapable of maintaining my prestige of position. Death or worse hovered over me. My life depended on regaining my precious garment and its contents. Who could have taken it? What could have been their object? And instantly the truth flashed upon my mind. It was that rascally high priest. He had seen me take pipe, tobacco and matches from my coat pocket. He had watched me narrowly, perhaps had kept his eyes upon me through some hidden peep-hole or opening, and had seen me remove my coat, and white I slept had seized it. Or perhaps he had ordered Zip to secure it for him. It made little difference which, for if it were in his possession he would have me in his power. He could order by fair means or foul, and knowing that every second I delayed increased my peril, I rushed to the ladder and across the roofs to the throne room.

From beneath me, as I started to descent, came the sounds of the hissing language in excited tones, and as my head came below the level of the roof my heart sank. The dark air of the room was heavy with tobacco smoke!

The next instant my feet were jerked from beneath me, I was seized, tumbled on the floor, and before I could strike or rise I was bound hand and foot. Dazed, startled and helpless I glanced about. Surrounding me were a dozen of the repulsive dwarfs. Gathered about the sides of the room were crowds of people, and seated upon the throne, puffing great clouds of smoke from my pipe, a wicked lear upon his ugly face, and thoroughly enjoying himself, was the priest, while beside him the king coughed and sneezed and looked very miserable.

All this I took in at a glance. Then I was seized and dragged roughly before the throne. I fully realized my doom was sealed. I was no longer a supernatural being to be feared and adored— my treatment proved that— but merely a prisoner, an ordinary mortal. Oddly enough, however, I was no longer frightened. My first fears had given place to anger, and I raged and fumed and prayed that the grinning fiend before me might be stricken with all the torturing sickness, which usually follows the beginner's first smoke.

But apparently he was immune to the effects, and as soon as I was dragged before the throne he rose, and pointing at me, addressed the crowd before him. That he was denouncing me as an imposter and at the same time tremendously increasing his own importance was evident by his tones, his gestures and the expression on his dark face. Moreover, he had another card to play. Pointing upward and waving his arm and making quite creditable imitation of an airplane's exhaust, he spoke vehemently and then pointed to a man who crouched on the dais.

At first I was at a loss to grasp his meaning, and then, as the trembling creature beside the throne spoke in frightened tones and gesticulated vividly, I realized he was the chap I had bumped into upon my arrival. He had spilled the beans and had informed the old scarecrow of a priest, that I had arrived via the tunnel and not from the sky.

I felt sure now that my doom was sealed. But there was nothing I could do or say. There was one chance in a million that I might be escorted from the valley and turned loose in the tunnel; but that gave me no comfort, for I knew that hideous certain death awaited me on that slope covered with the devilish man-eating-trees.

The chances, however, were all in favor of my being tortured and butchered. Strangely enough my greatest regret, the matter which troubled me the most and made me curse my carelessness in removing my coat while I slept, was not that I should be killed —I had faced death too often for that

—but the fact that I would be unable to report the wonderful discoveries I had made or give my knowledge of the city and its people to the world. Indeed, my thoughts were so concentrated on this that I gave little attention to the priest, until he stepped forward, and, with a nasty grimace, struck me savagely across the face. Maddened at the blow I lunged forward like a butting ram. My head struck squarely in the pit of his stomach, and with a gasping yell he doubled up and fell sprawling on the dais while the pipe flew from his lips and scattered its contents far and near. Before I could roll to one side, my guards seized and pulled me across the room. Despite my plight and the fate in store for me I laughed loudly and heartily as I saw the priest with hands pressed to stomach, eyes rolling wildly and a sickly greenish pallor on his face. The blow plus the tobacco had done its work. I had evened the score a bit at any rate.

The next moment I was hauled through a low doorway hidden by draperies, and, bumping like a bag of meal over the rough stones, was pitched into an inky black cell. Bruised, scratched and bleeding I lay there unable to move or see while the occasional sounds of shuffling footsteps, or rather handsteps, told me a guard was close at hand. For hour after hour I lay motionless, expecting each minute that I would be dragged out to torture or death and wondering dully what form it would take, until at last—numb, exhausted and worn out, I lost consciousness.

I was brought to my senses by being seized and jerked to a sitting posture, and found the cell illuminated by a spluttering torch, while two of the men supported my shoulders and a third held a gourd of water to my lips. My throat was parched and the liquid was most welcome, and a moment later, a fourth man appeared with food. It was evident that the priest had no intention of letting me die of thirst or starvation, and I wondered why he should be so solicitous of my comfort if I were doomed to an early death.

As soon as I had eaten, the guards withdrew, taking the torch, and I was once more left in stygian blackness with my thoughts. I wondered whether it were day or night, but I had no means of judging. It had been the middle of the afternoon when I had missed my coat, and, reasoning that the food served was probably the evening meal, I decided that it was now about sundown. In that case I should probably be put out of the way the next morning. That would be a full twenty-four hours before Hazen was due and I wondered what he would think when he saw no sign of me in the valley—whether he would surmise that I had not reached the city and had been killed by the Kunas, and what he would report to my friends in Colon.

But Colon, friends and Hazen seemed very far away as I thought of them there in that black hole awaiting death at the hands of the strange black dwarfs and, as far as any aid they could give me, was concerned I might well have been in Mars.

My thoughts were interrupted by my guards reappearing with the torch. Lifting me to my feet they loosened the bonds about my legs and urged me through a small doorway, where I was compelled to bend low to pass, and along a winding, narrow, low-ceilinged stone tunnel. That I was on my way to my execution I was sure, and vague thoughts of selling my life dearly and of overpowering my puny guards crossed my mind. But I dismissed such ideas as useless, for even were I to succeed I would be no better off. There were thousands of the tiny men in the city, it was impossible to escape from the valley unseen, and I had not the least idea where the underground passage led. To attempt to escape meant certain death, and there still remained a faint chance, a dim hope that I might yet be spared and merely deported. So, ducking my head and with stooping shoulders, I picked my way along the tunnel by the fitful glare of the flaming torch.

For what seemed miles the way led on and I began to think that the entrance was outside the valley and that was being led to freedom, when a glimmer of light showed ahead, the floor sloped upward, and, an instant later, I emerged in the open air.

For a moment my eyes were blinded by the light after the darkness of the passage and I could not grasp where I was. I had thought it evening, but I knew the night had passed and another day had come. Then, as I looked about at my surroundings and it dawned upon me where I was, a shudder of horror, a chill of deadly fear swept over me. I was on the summit of the pyramid. The sacrificial altar was within three paces. Beside it stood the fiendish priest and his assistants, and gathered upon the green plain were hordes of people with faces upturned towards me. I was about to be sacrificed, to be bound fast to the bloodstained awful stone, to have my still-beating heart torn from my living body!

Anything were preferable to that and with a sudden bound I strove to gain the altar's edge and hurl myself to certain death. But to no avail. Two of the dwarfs held me fast by the cord which fastened my wrists and I was jerked back to fall heavily upon the stones. Before I could struggle up, four of the priest's assistants sprang forward and, grasping me by legs and shoulders, lifted me and tossed me upon the stinking sacrificial stone. I was helpless, and instantly my ankles were tied fast to the metal staples, the bonds of my wrists were severed, my arms were drawn apart and securely lashed to other staples, the stone collar was placed about my neck forcing my head far back and I was ready for the glowering priest to wreak his awful vengeance.

Stepping close to the altar he drew a glittering obsidian knife—and even in my terrible predicament I noted this, and realized that he was adhering strictly to Aztec customs—and, raising his arms, he began a wailing, blood-curdling chant. Up from the thousands of throats below came the chanting chorus, rising and falling like a great wave of sound. How long I wondered, would this keep on? How much longer must this agony, this torture of suspense be borne? Why did he not strike his stone dagger into my chest and have it over with?

And then, from some dormant cell in my brain, came the answer. I was to be sacrificed to the sun god, and I remembered that, according to the Aztec religion, the blow could not be struck until the rising sun cast its rays upon the victim's chest above the heart. The priest was awaiting that moment. He was delaying until the sun, still behind the crater's rim, should throw its first rays upon me.

How long would it be? How many minutes must pass before the fatal finger of light pointed to my heart? With a mighty effort I turned my head slightly towards the east. Above the rugged mountain edge was a blaze of light. Even as I looked with aching eyes a golden beam shot across the valley and flashed blindingly into my face. It was now only a matter of seconds. The priest raised his knife aloft. The chant from the multitude ceased and over city and valley fell an ominous, awful silence. Upon the sacrificial knife the sun gleamed brilliantly, transforming the glass-like stone to burnished gold. With his free hand the priest tore open my shirt and bared my bosom. I felt that the end had come. I closed my eyes. And then, at the very instant when the knife was about to sweep down, faint and far away, like the humming of a giant bee, I caught a sound. It was unmistakable unlike anything else in all the world—the exhaust of an airplane's engines!

And my straining ears were not the only ones that heard that note. Over the priest's face swept a look of deadly fear. The poised knife was slowly lowered. He turned trembling towards the west and from the waiting throng below rose a mighty sigh of terror.

A new hope sprang up in my breast. Was it Hazen? He was not due until the next day and it might be only some army plane that would pass far to one side of the valley. No, the sound was increasing, the plane was approaching. But even were it Hazen would it help me any? Would he see my plight and descend or would he fly too far above the city to note what was taking place? For a space my life was saved. The fear of that giant, roaring bird would prevent the sacrifice. The priest feared he had made a mistake, that I was a god, that, from the sky, vengeance would swoop upon him and his people for the contemplated butchery. But if the plane passed? Or would his dread of it be greater than his fear of defying the sun god by failing in the sacrifice?

Now the roar of the motor sounded directly overhead and the next moment I glimpsed the plane speeding across the blue morning sky. Then it was gone. The exhaust grew fainter and fainter. All hope was lost. Whoever it was had flown on, all unsuspecting the awful fate of a fellow man upon that sunlit pyramid.

And now the priest was again towering over me. Once more he raised his knife. I could feel the warm sun beating upon my throat and shoulders. I could feel it creeping slowly but surely downward. The knife quivered in the impatient hand of the priest, I saw his muscles tense themselves for the blow, I caught the grim smile that flitted across his face as he prepared to strike.

An instant more and my palpitating heart would be held aloft for all to see.

But the blow never fell. With a deafening roar, that drowned the mighty shout of terror from the people, the airplane swooped like an eagle from the sky and clove the air within a hundred feet of the altar. With a gurgling cry the priest flung himself face down, and his knife fell clattering with the sound of broken glass upon the stones.

Was it Hazen? Would he see me? Would he alight? Was I saved?

The answer was a thunderous, fear maddened cry from below, a swishing whirr as of a gale of wind and a dark shadow sweeping over me.

And then my overwrought senses, my frazzled nerves could stand no more and all went black before my eyes.

Dimly consciousness came back. I heard the sounds of rushing feet, the panting labored breath of men, sharp, half uttered exclamations and terror and a deep drawn sigh of relief. Above my wondering eyes a figure suddenly loomed. A weird uncanny figure with strangely smooth and rounded head and great goggling, glassy eyes. With a jerk the stone collar was lifted from my strained neck and as full consciousness came back I gasped. It was Hazen! By some miracle he was ahead of time!

From somewhere, muffled behind that grotesque mask, came a hoarse: "My God, are you hurt?

Before I could speak the bonds were slashed from my ankles and wrists. A strong arm raised me and pulled me from the slab.

"For God's sake, hurry!" cried Hazen, as ha if supporting me he rushed toward the altar stairs. "I've got 'em buffaloed for a minute, but the Lord alone knows how long it'll hold 'em."

Rapidly as my numbed limbs would permit I rushed down the sloping, spiral way. Half carried by Hazen I raced across the few yards of grass between the base of the pyramid and the plane, and as I did so I caught a fleeting glimpse of a huddled, shapeless, bloody bundle of green and white. It was all that remained of the priest whom Hazen had hurled from the altar top!

The next moment I was in the plane and Hazen was twirling the propeller. There was a roar as the motor started. Hazen leaped like an acrobat to his seat and slowly the machine moved across the plain.

Everywhere the people were prostrate, but as the machine started forward one after another glanced up. Ere we had traveled a score of yards the creatures were rising and with frightful screams were scattering from our pathway. It was impossible to avoid them. With sickening shocks the whirring propeller struck one after another. Blood spattered our faces and becrimsoned the windshield and the wings. But uninjured the plane gathered headway; the uneven bumping over the ground ceased; we were traveling smoothly, lifting from the earth.

Then with a strange wild roar the people rushed for us. Racing on their hands they came. Rocks and missiles whizzed about us. An arrow whirred by my head and struck quivering in a strut. But now we were rising rapidly. We were looking down upon the maddened hosts, their arrows and sling-flung stones were striking the under surface of the fuselage and wings. We were safe at last. A moment more and we would be above the crater rim.

A sudden exclamation from Hazen startled me. I glanced up. Straight ahead rose the precipitous mountain side above the quarry. To clear it we must ascent far more rapidly than we I were doing.

"Must have splintered the blades!" jerked out Hazen. "She's not making it. Can't swing her. Rudder's jammed. Heave out everything you can find. Hurry or we'll smash!"

Before us loomed the ragged, rocky wall. We were rushing to our doom at lightning speed. At Hazen's words I grasped whatever I could find and tossed it over the side. A box of provisions, a roll of tools, a leather jacket, a thermos bottle, canteens, an automatic pistol and a cartridge belt all went, I glanced up. We were rising, faster. A few pounds more overboard, a few feet higher and we would be clear. Was there anything else I could throw out? Frantically I searched. I saw a can-like object resting on a frame. Spare gasoline I decided, but fuel was of no value now. With an effort I dragged it out. I lifted and hurled it over.

With a sudden jerk the plane sprung upward. There was a terrific muffled roar from below and with barely a yard to spare we rose above the crater rim.

"Lord, you must have dropped that old bomb!" cried Hazen. "The concussion jarred the rudder free."

I glanced over the side. Far beneath, a cloud of smoke and dust was drifting slowly aside exposing the aqueduct, broken smashed and in ruins. From the opening in the mountain side a mighty stream of water was roaring in a rushing, tearing torrent. The bomb had landed squarely in the quarry. The aqueduct had fallen, the shock had let loose the gates of the lake and the whole vast crater reservoir was pouring in a mighty flood across the valley.

In a wide arc Hazen swung the plane about. "Poor devils!"

he muttered as we soared above the doomed city.

Already the green plain was shimmering with the glint of water. We could see the frantic, frenzied people running and scrambling up their ladders. Again we wheeled and circled far above them and now only the-roof tops of the houses were above the flood. Presently these too sank from sight and above the sunlit waters only the sacrificial stone remained.

"It's all over!" exclaimed Hazen, and heading northward we sped beyond the encircling mountain sides. Beneath us now was forest, and with a shudder I recognized it as that death-dealing, nightmare grove of cannibal trees. Fascinated I gazed down and suddenly from the mountain side behind us burst a frothing yellow torrent. The pressure of the flood had been too great. The overwhelming waters had forced the stone door of the tunnel by which I had entered that incredible valley. Before my wondering eyes the devastating deluge swept down the slope. I saw the monstrous trees shiver and sway and crash before the irresistible force. They gave way and like matchsticks went tossing, tumbling, bobbing down the hillside.

Higher and higher we rose. The water-filled crater was now but a silvery lake. The slope up which I had fought and raced from the ravenous, blood-sucking trees was bare, red earth scarred deep by the plunging stream that flowed over it. Far to the west gleamed the blue Pacific. Like a vast map Darien was spread below us. Northward we sped. Before us was civilization. Behind us death and destruction. The man-eating trees were a thing of the past. The lost city was lost forever.

The RUNAWAY SKYSCRAPER

By Murray Leinster

...And before the wigwam were two or three Indians, utterly petrified with astonishment. Behind the first wigwam were others, painted like the first with daubs of brightly colored clay. From them, too, Indians issued, and stared in incredulous amazement, their eyes growing wider and wider.

Introduction

WE have all heard of and read about the Einstein, theory, which involves the use in its calculations of the mysterious "fourth dimension." Here our author gives a wonderfully effective picture of what the fourth dimension did in the annihilation of time, in the wiping out of the centuries, where it brings a company of twentieth century business men and women to a time centuries back from the days of modern New York—they are transferred with great rapidity of receding time to the days when Indians were the only inhabitants of Manhattan, until at last the recession of the centuries ceases and gives them pause for a while. The modern skyscraper has accompanied them on their way, but problems of food and support have to be worked out for them in their new position in the ages. At last they evolve a way to return, to get their skyscraper back to familiar old Madison Square. Read and see how they do it.

THE RUNAWAY SKYSCRAPER

By Murray Leinster

THE whole thing started when the clock on the Metropolitan Tower began to run backward. It was not a graceful proceeding. The hands had been moving onward in their customary deliberate fashion, slowly and thoughtfully, but suddenly the people in the offices near the clock's face heard an ominous creaking and groaning. There was a slight, hardly discernible shiver through the tower, and then something gave with a crash. The big hands on the clock began to move backward.

Immediately after the crash all the creaking and groaning ceased, and instead, the usual quiet again hung over everything. One or two of the occupants of the upper offices put their heads out into the halls, but the elevators were running as usual, the lights were burning, and all seemed calm and peaceful. The clerks and stenographers went back to their ledgers and typewriters, the business callers returned to the discussion of their errands, and the ordinary course of business was resumed.

Arthur Chamberlain was dictating a letter to Estelle Woodward, his sole stenographer. When the crash came he paused, listened, and then resumed his task.

It was not a difficult one. Talking to Estelle Woodward was at no time an onerous duty, but it must be admitted that Arthur Chamberlain found it difficult to keep his conversation strictly upon his business.

He was at this time engaged in dictating a letter to his principal creditors, the Gary & Milton Company, explaining that their demand for the immediate payment of the installment then due upon his office furniture was untimely and unjust. A young and budding engineer in New York never has too much money, and when he is young as Arthur Chamberlain was, and as fond of pleasant company, and not too fond of economizing, he is liable to find all demands for payment untimely and he usually considers them unjust as well. Arthur finished dictating the letter and sighed.

"Miss Woodward," he said regretfully, "I am afraid I shall never make a successful man."

Miss Woodward shook her head vaguely. She did not seem to take his remark very seriously, but then, she had learned never to take any of his remarks seriously. She had been puzzled at first by his manner of treating everything with a half-joking pessimism, but now ignored it.

She was interested in her own problems. She had suddenly decided that she was going to be an old maid, and it bothered her. She had discovered that she did not like any one well enough to marry, and she was in her twenty-second year.

She was not a native of New York, and the few young men she had met there she did not care for. She had regretfully decided she was too finicky, too fastidious, but could not seem to help herself. She could not understand their absorption in boxing and baseball and she did not like the way they danced.

She had considered the matter and decided that she would have to reconsider her former opinion of women who did not marry. Heretofore she had thought there must be something the matter with them. Now she believed that she would come to their own estate, and probably for the same reason. She could not fall in love and she wanted to.

She read all the popular novels and thrilled at the love-scenes contained in them, but when any of the young men she knew became in the slightest degree sentimental she found herself bored, and disgusted with herself for being bored. Still, she could not help it, and was struggling to reconcile herself to a life without romance.

She was far too pretty for that, of course, and Arthur Chamberlain often longed to tell her how pretty she really was, but her abstracted air held him at arms' length.

He lay back at ease in his swivel-chair and considered, looking at her with unfeigned pleasure. She did not notice it, for she was so much absorbed in her own thoughts that she rarely noticed anything he said or did when they were not in the line of her duties.

"Miss Woodward," he repeated, "I said I think I'll never

make a successful man. Do you know what that means?"

She looked at him mutely, polite inquiry in her eyes.

"It means," he said gravely, "that I'm going broke. Unless something turns up in the next three weeks, or a month at the latest, I'll have to get a job."

"And that means—" she asked.

"All this will go to pot," he explained with a sweeping gesture. "I thought I'd better tell you as much in advance as I could."

"You mean you're going to give up your office—and me?" she asked, a little alarmed.

"Giving up you will be the harder of the two," he said with a smile, "but that's what it means. You'll have no difficulty finding a new place, with three weeks in which to look for one, but I'm sorry."

"I'm sorry, too, Mr. Chamberlain," she said, her brow puckered.

She was not really frightened, because she knew she could get another position, but she became aware of rather more regret than she had expected.

There was silence for a moment.

"Jove!" said Arthur, suddenly. "It's getting dark, isn't it?"

It was. It was growing dark with unusual rapidity. Arthur went to his window, and looked out.

"Funny," he remarked in a moment or two. "Things don't look just right, down there, somehow. There are very few people about."

He watched in growing amazement. Lights came on in the streets below, but none of the buildings lighted up. It grew darker and darker.

"It shouldn't be dark at this hour!" Arthur exclaimed.

Estelle went to the window by his side.

"It looks awfully queer," she agreed. "It must be an eclipse or something."

They heard doors open in the hall outside, and Arthur ran out. The halls were beginning to fill with excited people.

"What on earth's the matter?" asked a worried stenographer.

"Probably an eclipse," replied Arthur. "Only it's odd we didn't read about it in the papers."

He glanced along the corridor. No one else seemed better informed than he, and he went back into his office.

Estelle turned from the window as he appeared.

"The streets are deserted," she said in a puzzled tone. "What's the matter? Did you hear?"

Arthur shook his head and reached for the telephone.

"I'll call up and find out," he said confidently. He held the receiver to his ear. "What the—" he exclaimed. "Listen to this!"

A small-sized roar was coming from the receiver. Arthur hung up and turned a blank face upon Estelle.

"Look!" she said suddenly, and pointed out of the window.

All the city was now lighted up, and such of the signs as they could see were brilliantly illumined. They watched in silence. The streets once more seemed filled with vehicles. They darted along, their headlamps lighting up the roadway brilliantly. There was, however, something strange even about their motion. Arthur and Estelle watched in growing amazement and perplexity.

"Are—are you seeing what I am seeing?" asked Estelle breathlessly. "*I* see them *going backward*!"

Arthur watched, and collapsed into a chair.

"For the love of Mike!" he exclaimed softly.

The Rotation of the Earth Reversed

HE was roused by another exclamation from Estelle.

"It's getting light again," she said.

Arthur rose and went eagerly to the window. The darkness was becoming less intense, but in a way Arthur could hardly credit.

Far to the west, over beyond the Jersey hills—easily visible from the height at which Arthur's office was located—a faint light appeared in the sky, grew stronger and then took on a reddish tint. That, in turn, grew deeper, and at last the sun appeared, rising unconcernedly *in the west.*

Arthur gasped. The streets below continued to be thronged with people and motor-cars. The sun was traveling with extraordinary rapidity. It rose overhead, and as if by magic the streets were thronged with people. Every one seemed to be running at top-speed. The few teams they saw moved at a breakneck pace—backward! In spite of the suddenly topsyturvy state of affairs there seemed to be no accidents.

Arthur put his hands to his head.

"Miss Woodward," he said pathetically, "I'm afraid I've gone crazy. Do you see the same things I do?"

Estelle nodded. Her eyes wide open.

"What *is* the matter?" she asked helplessly.

She turned again to the window. The square was almost empty once more. The motor-cars still traveling about the streets were going so swiftly they were hardly visible. Their speed seemed to increase steadily. Soon it was almost impossible to distinguish them, and only a grayish blur marked their paths along Fifth Avenue and Twenty-Third Street.

It grew dusk, and then rapidly dark. As their office was on the western side of the building they could not see that the sun had sunk in the east, but subconsciously they realized that this must be the case.

In silence they watched the panorama grow black except for the street-lamps, remain thus for a time, and then suddenly spring into brilliantly illuminated activity.

Again this lasted for a little while, and the west once more began to glow. The sun rose somewhat more hastily from the Jersey hills and began to soar overhead, but very soon darkness fell again. With hardly an interval the city became illuminated, and then the west grew red once more.

"Apparently," said Arthur, steadying his voice with a conscious effort, "there's been a cataclysm somewhere, the direction of the earth's rotation has been reversed, and its speed immensely increased. It seems to take only about five minutes for a rotation now."

As he spoke darkness fell for the third time. Estelle turned from the window with a white face.

"What's going to happen?" she cried.

"I don't know," answered Arthur. "The scientist fellows tell us if the earth were to spin fast enough the centrifugal force would throw us all off into space. Perhaps that's what's going to happen."

Estelle sank into a chair and stared at him, appalled. There was a sudden explosion behind them. With a start, Estelle jumped to her feet and turned. A little gilt clock over her typewriter-desk lay in fragments. Arthur hastily glanced at his own watch.

"Great bombs and little cannon-balls!" he shouted. "Look at this!"

His watch trembled and quivered in his hand. The hands were going around so swiftly it was impossible to watch the minute-hand, and the hour-hand traveled like the wind.

While they looked, it made two complete revolutions. In

one of them the glory of daylight had waxed, waned, and vanished. In the other, darkness reigned except for the glow from the electric light overhead.

There was a sudden tension and catch in the watch. Arthur dropped it instantly. It flew to pieces before it reached the floor.

"If you've got a watch," Arthur ordered swiftly, "stop it this instant!"

Estelle fumbled at her wrist. Arthur tore the watch from her hand and threw open the case. The machinery inside was going so swiftly it was hardly visible; Relentlessly, Arthur jabbed a penholder in the works. There was a sharp click, and the watch was still.

Arthur ran to the window. As he reached it the sun rushed up, day lasted a moment, there was darkness, and then the sun appeared again.

"Miss Woodward!" Arthur ordered suddenly, "look at the ground!"

Estelle glanced down. The next time the sun flashed into view she gasped.

The ground was white with snow!

"What *has* happened?" she demanded, terrified. "Oh, what *has* happened?"

Arthur fumbled at his chin awkwardly, watching the astonishing panorama outside. There was hardly any distinguishing between the times the sun was up and the times it was below now, as the darkness and light followed each other so swiftly the effect was the same as one of the old flickering motion-pictures.

As Arthur watched, this effect became more pronounced. The tall Fifth Avenue Building across the way began to disintegrate. In a moment, it seemed, there was only a skeleton there. Then that vanished, story by story. A great cavity in the earth appeared, and then another building became visible, a smaller, brown-stone, unimpressive structure.

With bulging eyes Arthur stared across the city. Except for the flickering, he could see almost clearly now.

He no longer saw the sun rise and set. There was merely a streak of unpleasantly brilliant light across the sky. Bit by bit, building by building, the city began to disintegrate and become replaced by smaller, dingier buildings. In a little while those began to disappear and leave gaps where they vanished.

Arthur strained his eyes and looked far down-town. He saw a forest of masts and spars along the waterfront for a moment and when he turned his eyes again to the scenery near him it was almost barren of houses, and what few showed were mean, small residences, apparently set in the midst of farms and plantations.

Estelle was sobbing.

"Oh, Mr. Chamberlain," she cried. "What is the matter? What has happened?"

Arthur had lost his fear of what their fate would be in his absorbing interest in what he saw. He was staring out of the window, wide-eyed, lost in the sight before him. At Estelle's cry, however, he reluctantly left the window and patted her shoulder awkwardly.

"I don't know how to explain it," he said uncomfortably, "but it's obvious that my first surmise was all wrong. The speed of the earth's rotation can't have been increased, because if it had to the extent we see, we'd have been thrown off into space long ago. But—have you read anything about the Fourth Dimension?"

Estelle shook her head hopelessly.

"Well, then, have you ever read anything by Wells? The 'Time Machine,' for instance?"

Again she shook her head.

"I don't know how I'm going to say it so you'll understand, but time is just as much a dimension as length and breadth. From what I can judge, I'd say there has been an earthquake, and the ground has settled a little with our building on it, only instead of settling down toward the center of the earth, or side-wise, it's settled in this fourth dimension."

"But what does that mean?" asked Estelle uncomprehendingly.

"If the earth had settled down, we'd have been lower. If it had settled to one side, we'd have been moved one way or another, but as it's settled back in the Fourth Dimension, we're going back in time."

"Then—"

"We're in a runaway skyscraper, bound for some time back before the discovery of America!"

The Seasons Are Reversed in Order

IT was very still in the office. Except for the flickering outside everything seemed very much as usual. The electric light burned steadily, but Estelle was sobbing with fright and Arthur was trying vainly to console her.

"Have I gone crazy?" she demanded between her sobs.

"Not unless I've gone mad, too," said Arthur soothingly. The excitement had quite a soothing effect upon him. He had ceased to feel afraid, but was simply waiting to see what had happened. "We're way back before the founding of New York now, and still going strong."

"Are you sure that's what has happened?"

"If you'll look outside," he suggested, "you'll see the

seasons following each other in reverse order. One moment the snow covers all the ground, then you catch a glimpse of autumn foliage, then summer follows, and next spring."

Estelle glanced out of the window and covered her eyes.

"Not a house," she said despairingly. "Not a building. Nothing, nothing, nothing!"

Arthur slipped, his arm about her and patted hers comfortingly.

"It's all right," he reassured her. "We'll bring up presently, and there we'll be. There's nothing to be afraid of."

She rested her head on his shoulder and sobbed hopelessly for a little while longer, but presently quieted. Then, suddenly, realizing that Arthur's arm was about her and that she was crying on his shoulder, she sprang away, blushing crimson.

Arthur walked to the window.

"Look there!" he exclaimed, but it was too late. "I'll swear to it I saw the Half Moon, Hudson's ship," he declared excitedly. "We're way back now, and don't seem to be slacking up, either."

Estelle came to the window by his side. The rapidly changing scene before her made her gasp. It was no longer possible to distinguish night from day.

A wavering streak, moving first to the right and then to the left, showed where the sun flashed across the sky.

"What makes the sun wobble so?" she asked.

"Moving north and south of the equator," Arthur explained casually. "When it's farthest south—to the left—there's always snow on the ground. When it's farthest right it's summer. See how green it is?"

A few moments' observation corroborated his statement.

"I'd say," Arthur remarked reflectively, "that it takes about fifteen seconds for the sun to make the round trip from farthest north to farthest south." He felt his pulse. "Do you know the normal rate of the heart-beat? We can judge time that way. A clock will go all to pieces, of course."

"Why did your watch explode—and the clock?"

"Running forward in time unwinds a clock, doesn't it?" asked Arthur. "It follows, of course, that when you move it backward in time it winds up. When you move it too far back, you wind it so tightly that the spring just breaks to pieces."

He paused a moment, his fingers on his pulse.

"Yes, it takes about fifteen seconds for all the four seasons to pass. That means we're going backward in time about four years a minute. If we go on at this rate another hour we'll be back in the time of the Northmen, and will be able to tell if they did discover America, after all."

"Funny we don't hear any noises," Estelle observed. She had caught some of Arthur's calmness.

"It passes so quickly that though our ears hear it, we don't separate the sounds. If you'll notice, you do hear a sort of humming. It's very high-pitched, though."

Estelle listened, but could hear nothing.

"No matter," said Arthur. "It's probably a little higher than your ears will catch. Lots of people can't hear a bat squeak."

"I never could," said Estelle. "Out in the country, where I come from, other people could hear them, but I couldn't."

They stood a while in silence, watching.

"When are we going to stop?" asked Estelle uneasily. "It seems as if we're going to keep on indefinitely."

"I guess we'll stop all right," Arthur reassured her. "It's obvious that whatever it was, only affected our own building, or we'd see some other one with us. It looks like a fault or a flaw in the rock the building rests on. And that can only give so far."

Estelle was silent for a moment.

"Oh, I can't be sane!" she burst out semihysterically. "This can't be happening!"

"You aren't crazy," said Arthur sharply. "You're sane as I am. Just something queer is happening. Buck up. Say your multiplication tables. Say anything you know. Say something sensible and you'll know you're all right. But don't get frightened now. There'll be plenty to get frightened about later."

The grimness in his tone alarmed Estelle.

"What are you afraid of?" she asked quickly.

"Time enough to worry when it happens," Arthur retorted briefly.

"You—you aren't afraid we'll go back before the beginning of the world, are you?" asked Estelle in sudden access of fright.

Arthur shook his head.

"Tell me," said Estelle more quietly, getting a grip on herself. "I won't mind. But please tell me."

Arthur glanced at her. Her face was pale, but there was more resolution in it than he had expected to find.

"I'll tell you, then," he said reluctantly. "We're going back a little faster than we were, and the flaw seems to be a deeper one than I thought. At the roughest kind of an estimate, we're all of a thousand years before the discovery of America now, and I think nearer three or four. And we're gaining speed all the time. So, though I am as sure as I can be sure of anything that we'll stop this cave-in eventually, I don't know where. It's like a crevasse in the earth opened by an earthquake which may be only a few feet deep, or it may be hundreds of yards, or even a mile or two. We started off smoothly. We're going at a terrific rate. *What will happen when we stop?*"

Estelle caught her breath.

"What?" she asked quietly.

"I don't know," said Arthur in an irritated tone, to cover his apprehension. "How could I know?"

Estelle turned from him to the window again.

"Look!" she said, pointing.

The flickering had begun again. While they stared, hope springing up once more in their hearts, it became more pronounced. Soon they could distinctly see the difference between day and night.

They were slowing up! The white snow on the ground remained there for an appreciable time, autumn lasted quite a while. They could catch the flashes of the sun as it made its revolutions now, instead of its seeming like a ribbon of fire. At last day lasted all of fifteen or twenty minutes.

It grew longer and longer. Then half an hour, then an hour. The sun wavered in midheaven and was still.

Far below them, the watchers in the tower of the skyscraper saw trees swaying and bending in the wind. Though there was not a house or a habitation to be seen and a dense forest covered all of Manhattan Island, such of the world as they could see looked normal. Wherever or rather in whatever epoch of time they were, they had arrived.

Indians Occupy Madison Square

ARTHUR caught at Estelle's arm and the two made a dash for the elevators. Fortunately one was standing still, the door open, on their floor. The elevator-boy had deserted his post and was looking with all the rest of the occupants of the building at the strange landscape that surrounded them.

No sooner had the pair reached the car, however, than the boy came hurrying along the corridor, three or four other people following him also at a run. Without a word the boy rushed inside, the others crowded after him, and the car shot downward, all of the newcomers panting from their sprint.

Theirs was the first car to reach the bottom. They rushed out and to the western door.

Here, where they had been accustomed to see Madison Square spread out before them, a clearing of perhaps half an acre in extent showed itself. Where their eyes instinctively looked for the dark bronze fountain, near which soap-box orators aforetime held sway, they saw a tent, a wigwam of hides and bark gaily painted. And before the wigwam were two or three Indians, utterly petrified with astonishment.

Behind the first wigwam were others, painted like the first with daubs of brightly colored clay. From them, too, Indians issued, and stared in incredulous amazement, their eyes growing wider and wider. When the group of white people confronted the Indians there was a moment's deathlike silence. Then, with a wild yell, the redskins broke and ran, not stopping to gather together their belongings, nor pausing for even a second glance at the weird strangers who invaded their domain.

Arthur took two or three deep breaths of the fresh air and found himself even then comparing its quality with that of the city. Estelle stared about her with unbelieving eyes. She turned and saw the great bulk of the office building behind her, then faced this small clearing with a virgin forest on its farther side.

She found herself trembling from some undefined cause. Arthur glanced at her. He saw the trembling and knew she would have a fit of nerves in a moment if something did not come up demanding instant attention.

"We'd better take a look at this village," he said in an offhand voice. "We can probably find out how long ago it is from the weapons and so on."

He grasped her arm firmly and led her in the direction of the tents. The other people, left behind, displayed their emotions in different ways. Two or three of them—women—sat frankly down on the steps and indulged in tears of bewilderment, fright and relief in a peculiar combination defying analysis. Two or three of the men swore, in shaken voices.

Meantime, the elevators inside the building were rushing and clanging, and the hall filled with a white-faced mob, desperately anxious to find out what had happened and why. The people poured out of the door and stared about blankly. There was a peculiar expression of doubt on every one of their faces. Each one was asking himself if he were awake, and having proved that by pinches, openly administered, the next query was whether they had gone mad.

Arthur led Estelle cautiously among the tents.

The village contained about a dozen wigwams. Most of them were made of strips of birch-bark, cleverly overlapping each other, the seams cemented with gum. All had hide flaps for doors, and one or two were built almost entirely of hides, sewed together with strips of sinew.

Arthur made only a cursory examination of the village. His principal motive in taking Estelle there was to give her some mental occupation to ward off the reaction from the excitement of the cataclysm.

He looked into one or two of the tents and found merely couches of hides, with minor domestic utensils scattered about. He brought from one tent a bow and quiver of arrows. The workmanship was good, but very evidently the maker had no knowledge of metal tools.

Arthur's acquaintance with archeological subjects was very slight, but he observed that the arrow-heads were chipped, and not rubbed smooth. They were attached to the shafts with strips of gut or tendon.

Arthur was still pursuing his investigation when a sob from Estelle made him stop and look at her.

"Oh, what are we going to do?" she asked tearfully. "What *are* we going to do? Where are we?"

"You mean, *when* are we," Arthur corrected with a grim smile. "I don't know. Way back before the discovery of America, though. You can see in everything in the village that there isn't a trace of European civilization. I suspect that we are several thousand years back. I can't tell, of course, but this pottery makes me think so. See this bowl?"

He pointed to a bowl of red clay lying on the ground before one of the wigwams.

"If you'll look, you'll see that it isn't really pottery at all. It's a basket that was woven of reeds and then smeared with clay to make it fire-resisting. The people who made that didn't know about baking clay to make it stay put. When America was discovered nearly all the tribes knew something about pottery."

"But what are we going to do?" Estelle tearfully insisted.

"We're going to muddle along as well as we can," answered Arthur cheerfully, "until we can get back to where we started from. Maybe the people back in the twentieth century can send a relief party after us. When the skyscraper vanished it must have left a hole of some sort, and it may be possible for them to follow us down."

"If that's so," said Estelle quickly, "why can't we climb up it without waiting for them to come after us?"

Arthur scratched his head. He looked across the clearing at

the skyscraper. It seemed to rest very solidly on the ground. He looked up. The sky seemed normal.

"To tell the truth," he admitted, "there doesn't seem to be any hole. I said that more to cheer you up than anything else."

Estelle clenched her hands tightly and took a grip on herself.

"Just tell me the truth," she said quietly. "I was rather foolish, but tell me what you honestly think."

Arthur eyed her keenly.

"In that case," he said reluctantly, "I'll admit we're in a pretty bad fix. I don't know what has happened, how it happened, or anything about it. I'm just going to keep on going until I see a way clear to get out of this mess. There are two thousand of us people, more or less, and among all of us we must be able to find a way out."

Estelle had turned very pale.

"We're in no great danger from Indians," went on Arthur thoughtfully, "or from anything else that I know of—except one thing."

"What is that?" asked Estelle quickly.

Arthur shook his head and led her back toward the skyscraper, which was now thronged with the people from all the floors who had come down to the ground and were standing excitedly about the concourse asking each other what had happened.

Arthur led Estelle to one of the corners.

"Wait for me here," he ordered. "I'm going to talk to this crowd."

He pushed his way through until he could reach the confectionery and news-stand in the main hallway. Here he climbed up on the counter and shouted:

"People, listen to me! I'm going to tell you what's happened!"

In an instant there was dead silence. He found himself the center of a sea of white faces, every one contorted with fear and anxiety.

"To begin with," he said confidently, "there's nothing to be afraid of. We're going to get back to where we started from! I don't know how, yet, but we'll do it. Don't get frightened. Now I'll tell you what's happened."

He rapidly sketched out for them, in words as simple as he could make them, his theory that a flaw in the rock on which the foundations rested had developed and let the skyscraper sink, not downward, but into the Fourth Dimension.

"I'm an engineer," he finished. "What nature can do, we can imitate. Nature let us into this hole. We'll climb out. In the mean time, matters are serious. We needn't be afraid of not getting back. We'll do that. What we've got to fight is—starvation!"

Planning For the Food Supply

"WE'VE got to fight starvation, and we've got to beat it," Arthur continued doggedly. "I'm telling you this right at the outset, because I want you to begin right at the beginning and pitch in to help. We have very little food and a lot of us to eat it. First, I want some volunteers to help with rationing. Next, I want every ounce of food, in this place put under guard where it can be served to those who need it most. Who will help out with this?"

The swift succession of shocks had paralyzed the faculties of most of the people there, but half a dozen moved forward. Among them was a single gray-haired man with an air of accustomed authority. Arthur recognized him as the president of the bank on the ground floor.

"I don't know who you are or if you're right in saying what has happened," said the gray-haired man. "But I see something's got to be done, and—well, for the time being I'll take your word for what that is. Later on we'll thrash this matter out."

Arthur nodded. He bent over and spoke in a low voice to the gray-haired man, who moved away.

"Grayson, Walters, Terhune, Simpson, and Forsythe come here," the gray-haired man called at a doorway.

A number of men began to press dazedly toward him. Arthur resumed his harangue.

"You people—those of you who aren't too dazed to think—are remembering there's a restaurant in the building and no need to starve. You're wrong. There are nearly two thousand of us here. That means six thousand meals a day. We've got to have nearly ten tons of food a day, and we've got to have it at once."

"Hunt?" some one suggested.

"I saw Indians," some one else shouted. "Can we trade with them?"

"We can hunt and we can trade with the Indians," Arthur admitted, "but we need food by the ton—by the ton, people! The Indians don't store up supplies, and, besides, they're much too scattered to have a surplus for us. But we've got to have food. Now, how many of you know anything about hunting, fishing, trapping, or any possible way of getting food?"

There were a few hands raised—pitifully few. Arthur saw Estelle's hand up.

"Very well," he said. "Those of you who raised your hands then come with me up on the second floor and we'll talk it over. The rest of you try to conquer your fright, and don't go outside for a while. We've got some things to attend to before it will be quite safe for you to venture out. And keep away from the restaurant. There are armed guards over that food. Before we pass it out indiscriminately, we'll see to it there's more for to-morrow and the next day."

He stepped down from the counter and moved toward the stairway. It was not worth while to use the elevator for the ride of only one floor. Estelle managed to join him, and they mounted the steps together.

"Do you think we'll pull through all right?" she asked quietly.

"We've got to!" Arthur told her, setting his chin firmly. "We've simply got to."

The gray-haired president of the bank was waiting for them at the top of the stairs.

"My name is Van Deventer," he said, shaking hands with Arthur, who gave his own name.

"Where shall our emergency council sit?" he asked.

"The bank has a board room right over the safety vault. I dare say we can accommodate everybody there—everybody in the council, anyway."

Arthur followed into the board-room, and the others trooped in after him.

"I'm just assuming temporary leadership," Arthur explained, "because it's imperative some things be done at once. Later on we can talk about electing officials to direct our activities. Right now we need food. How many of you can shoot?"

About a quarter of the hands were raised. Estelle's was among the number.

"And how many are fishermen?"

A few more went up.

"What do the rest of you do?"

There was a chorus of "gardener," "I have a garden in my yard," "I grow peaches in New Jersey," and three men confessed that they raised chickens as a hobby.

"We'll want you gardeners in a little while. Don't go yet. But the most important are huntsmen and fishermen. Have any of you weapons in your offices?"

A number had revolvers, but only one man had a shotgun and shells.

"I was going on my vacation this afternoon straight from the office," he explained, "and have all my vacation tackle."

"Good man!" Arthur exclaimed. "You'll go after the heavy game."

"With a shotgun?" the sportsman asked, aghast.

"If you get close to them a shotgun will do as well as anything, and we can't waste a shell on every bird or rabbit. Those shells of yours are precious. You other fellows will have to turn fishermen for a while. Your pistols are no good for hunting."

"The watchmen at the bank have riot guns," said Van Deventer, "and there are one or two repeating-rifles there. I don't know about ammunition."

"Good! I don't mean about the ammunition, but about the guns. We'll hope for the ammunition. You fishermen get to work to improvise tackle out of anything you can get hold of. Will you do that?"

A series of nods answered his question.

"Now for the gardeners. You people will have to roam through the woods in company with the hunters and locate anything in the way of edibles that grows. Do all of you know what wild plants look like? I mean wild fruits and vegetables that are good to eat."

A few of them nodded, but the majority looked dubious. The consensus of opinion seemed to be that they would try. Arthur seemed a little discouraged.

"I guess you're the man to tell about the restaurant," Van Deventer said quietly. "And as this is the food commission, or something of that sort, everybody here will be better for hearing it. Anyway, everybody will have to know it before night. I took over the restaurant as you suggested, and posted some of the men from the bank that I knew I could trust about the doors. But there was hardly any use in doing it."

"The restaurant stocks up in the afternoon, as most of its business is in the morning and at noon. It only carries a day's stock of foodstuffs, and the—the cataclysm, or whatever it was, came at three o'clock. There is practically nothing in the place. We couldn't make sandwiches for half the women that are caught with us, let alone the men. Everybody will go hungry to-night. There will be no breakfast to-morrow, nor anything to eat until we either make arrangements with the Indians for some supplies or else get food for ourselves."

Arthur leaned his jaw on his hand and considered. A slow flush crept over his cheek. He was getting his fighting blood up.

At school, when he began to flush slowly his schoolmates had known the symptom and avoided his wrath. Now he was growing angry with mere circumstances, but it would be none the less unfortunate for those circumstances.

"Well," he said at last deliberately, "we've got to—What's that?"

There was a great creaking and groaning. Suddenly a sort of vibration was felt under foot. The floor began to take on a slight slant.

"Great Heaven!" some one cried. "The building's turning

over and we'll be buried in the ruins!"

The tilt of the floor became more pronounced. An empty chair slid to one end of the room. There was a crash.

Arthur and Estelle in Conference

ARTHUR woke to find some one tugging at his shoulders, trying to drag him from beneath the heavy table, which had wedged itself across his feet and pinned him fast, while a flying chair had struck him on the head and knocked him unconscious.

"Oh, come and help," Estelle's voice was calling deliberately. "Somebody come and help! He's caught in here!"

She was sobbing in a combination of panic and some unknown emotion.

"Help me, please!" she gasped, then her voice broke despondently, but she never ceased to tug ineffectually at Chamberlain, trying to drag him out of the mass of wreckage.

Arthur moved a little, dazedly.

"Are you alive?" she called anxiously. "Are you alive? Hurry, oh, hurry and wriggle out. The building's falling to pieces!"

"I'm all right," Arthur said weakly. "You get out before it all comes down."

"I won't leave you," she declared "Where are you caught? Are you badly hurt? Hurry, please hurry!"

Arthur stirred, but could not loosen his feet. He half-rolled over, and the table moved as if it had been precariously balanced, and slid heavily to one side. With Estelle still tugging at him, he managed to get to his feet on the slanting floor and stared about him.

Arthur continued to stare about.

"No danger," he said weakly. "Just the floor of the one

room gave way. The aftermath of the rock-flaw."

He made his way across the splintered flooring and piled-up chairs.

"We're on top of the safe-deposit vault," he said. "That's why we didn't fall all the way to the floor below. I wonder how we're going to get down?"

Estelle followed him, still frightened for fear of the building falling upon them. Some of the long floor-boards stretched over the edge of the vault and rested on a tall, bronze grating that protected the approach to the massive strong-box. Arthur tested them with his foot.

"They seem to be pretty solid," he said tentatively.

His strength was coming back to him every moment. He had been no more than stunned. He walked out on the planking to the bronze grating and turned.

"If you don't get dizzy, you might come on," he said. "We can swing down the grille here to the floor."

Estelle followed gingerly and in a moment they were safely below. The corridor was quite empty.

"When the crash came," Estelle explained, her voice shaking with the reaction from her fear of a moment ago, "every one thought the building was coming to pieces, and ran out. I'm afraid they've all run away."

"They'll be back in a little while," Arthur said quietly.

They went along the big marble corridor to the same western door, out of which they had first gone to see the Indian village. As they emerged into the sunlight they met a few of the people who had already recovered from their panic and were returning.

A crowd of respectable size gathered in a few moments, all still pale and shaken, but coming back to the building which was their refuge. Arthur leaned wearily against the cold stone.

It seemed to vibrate under his touch. He turned quickly to Estelle.

"Feel this," he exclaimed.

She did so.

"I've been wondering what that rumble was," she said. "I've been hearing it ever since we landed here, but didn't understand where it came from."

"You hear a rumble?" Arthur asked, puzzled. "I can't hear anything."

"It isn't as loud as it was, but I hear it," Estelle insisted. "It's very deep, like the lowest possible bass note of an organ."

"You couldn't hear the shrill whistle when we were coming here," Arthur exclaimed suddenly, "and you can't hear the squeak of a bat. Of course your ears are pitched lower than usual, and you can hear sounds that are lower than I can hear. Listen carefully. Does it sound in the least like a liquid rushing through somewhere?"

"Y-yes," said Estelle hesitatingly. "Somehow, I don't quite understand how, it gives me the impression of a tidal flow or something of that sort."

Arthur rushed indoors. When Estelle followed him she found him excitedly examining the marble floor about the base of the vault.

"It's cracked," he said excitedly. "It's cracked! The vault rose all of an inch!"

Estelle looked and saw the cracks.

"What does that mean?"

"It means we're going to get back where we belong," Arthur cried jubilantly. "It means I'm on the track of the whole trouble. It means everything's going to be all right."

He prowled about the vault exultantly, noting exactly how the cracks in the flooring ran and seeing in each a corroboration of his theory.

"I'll have to make some inspections in the cellar," he went on happily, "but I'm nearly sure I'm on the right track and can figure out a corrective."

"How soon can we hope to start back?" asked Estelle eagerly.

Arthur hesitated, then a great deal of the excitement ebbed from his face, leaving it rather worried and stern.

"It may be a month, or two months, or a year," he answered gravely. "I don't know. If the first thing I try will work, it won't be long. If we have to experiment, I daren't guess how long we may be. But"—his chin set firmly—"we're going to get back."

Estelle looked at him speculatively. Her own expression grew a little worried, too.

"But in a month," she said dubiously, "we—there is hardly any hope of our finding food for two thousand people for a month, is there?"

"We've got to," Arthur declared. "We can't hope to get that much food from the Indians. It will be days before they'll dare to come back to their village, if they ever come. It will be weeks before we can hope to have them earnestly at work to feed us, and that's leaving aside the question of how we'll communicate with them, and how we'll manage to trade with them. Frankly, I think everybody is going to have to draw his belt tight before we get through—if we do. Some of us will get along, anyway."

Estelle's eyes opened wide as the meaning of his last sentence penetrated her mind.

"You mean—that all of us won't—"

"I'm going to take care of you," Arthur said gravely, "but there are liable to be lively doings around here when people begin to realize they're really in a tight fix for food. I'm going to get Van Deventer to help me organize a police band to enforce martial law. We mustn't have any disorder, that's certain, and I don't trust a city-bred man in a pinch unless I know him."

He stooped and picked up a revolver from the floor, left there by one of the bank watchmen when he fled, in the belief that the building was falling.

Wild Pigeons Dash Against the Building

ARTHUR stood at the window of his office and stared out toward the west. The sun was setting, but upon what a scene!

Where, from this same window Arthur had seen the sun setting behind the Jersey hills, all edged with the angular roofs of factories, with their chimneys emitting columns of smoke, he now saw the same sun sinking redly behind a mass of luxuriant foliage. And where he was accustomed to look upon the tops of high buildings—each entitled to the name of "skyscraper"—he now saw miles and miles of waving green branches.

The wide Hudson flowed on placidly, all unruffled by the arrival of this strange monument upon its shores—the same Hudson Arthur knew as a busy thoroughfare of puffing steamers and chugging launches. Two or three small streams wandered unconcernedly across the land that Arthur had known as the most closely built-up territory on earth. And far, far below him—Arthur had to lean well out of his window to see it—stood a collection of tiny wigwams. Those small bark structures represented the original metropolis of New York.

His telephone rang. Van Deventer was on the wire. The exchange in the building was still working. Van Deventer wanted Arthur to come down to his private office. There were still a great many things to be settled—the arrangements for commandeering offices for sleeping quarters for the women, and numberless other details. The men who seemed to have best kept their heads were gathering there to settle upon a course of action.

Arthur glanced out of the window again before going to the elevator. He saw a curiously compact dark cloud moving swiftly across the sky to the west.

"Miss Woodward," he said sharply, "What is that?"

Estelle came to the window and looked.

"They are birds," she told him. "Birds flying in a group. I've often seen them in the country, though never as many as that."

"How do you catch birds?" Arthur asked her. "I know about shooting them, and so on, but we haven't guns enough to count. Could we catch them in traps, do you think?"

"I wouldn't be surprised," said Estelle thoughtfully. "But it would be hard to catch many."

"Come down-stairs," directed Arthur. "You know as much as any of the men here, and more than most, apparently. We're going to make you show us how to catch things."

Estelle smiled, a trifle wanly. Arthur led the way to the elevator. In the car he noticed that she looked distressed.

"What's the matter?" he asked. "You aren't really frightened, are you?"

"No," she answered shakily, "but—I'm rather upset about this thing. It's so—so terrible, somehow, to be back here, thousands of miles, or years, away from all one's friends and everybody."

"Please"—Arthur smiled encouragingly at her—"please count me your friend, won't you?"

She nodded, but blinked back some tears. Arthur would have tried to hearten her further, but the elevator stopped at their floor. They walked into the room where the meeting of cool heads was to take place.

No more than a dozen men were in there talking earnestly but dispiritedly. When Arthur and Estelle entered Van Deventer came over to greet them.

"We've got to do something," he said in a low voice. "A wave of homesickness has swept over the whole place. Look at those men. Every one is thinking about his family and contrasting his cozy fireside with all that wilderness outside."

"You don't seem to be worried," Arthur observed with a smile.

Van Deventer's eyes twinkled.

"I'm a bachelor," he said cheerfully, "and I live in a hotel. I've been longing for a chance to see some real excitement for thirty years. Business has kept me from it up to now, but I'm enjoying myself hugely."

Estelle looked at the group of dispirited men.

"We'll simply have to do something," she said with a shaky smile. "I feel just as they do. This morning I hated the thought of having to go back to my boarding-house to-night, but right now I feel as if the odor of cabbage in the hallway would seem like heaven."

Arthur led the way to the flat-topped desk in the middle of the room.

"Let's settle a few of the more important matters," he said in a businesslike tone. "None of us has any authority to act for the rest of the people in the tower, but so many of us are in a state of blue funk that those who are here must have charge for a while. Anybody any suggestions?"

"Housing," answered Van Deventer promptly. "I suggest that we draft a gang of men to haul all the upholstered settees and rugs that are to be found to one floor, for the women to sleep on."

"M—m. Yes. That's a good idea. Anybody a better plan?"

No one spoke. They all still looked much too homesick to take any great interest in anything, but they began to listen more or less half-heartedly.

"I've been thinking about coal," said Arthur. "There's undoubtedly a supply in the basement, but I wonder if it wouldn't be well to cut the lights off most of the floors, only lighting up the ones we're using."

"That might be a good idea later," Estelle said quietly, "but light is cheering, somehow, and every one feels so blue that I wouldn't do it to-night. To-morrow they'll begin to get up their resolution again, and you can ask them to do things."

"If we're going to starve to death," one of the other men said gloomily, "we might as well have plenty of light to do it by."

"We aren't going to starve to death," retorted Arthur sharply. "Just before I came down I saw a great cloud of birds, greater than I had ever seen before. When we get at those birds—"

"When," echoed the gloomy one.

"They were pigeons," Estelle explained. "They shouldn't be hard to snare or trap."

"I usually have my dinner before now," the gloomy one protested, "and I'm told I won't get anything to-night."

The other men began to straighten their shoulders. The peevishness of one of their number seemed to bring out their latent courage.

"Well, we've got to stand it for the present," one of them

said almost philosophically. "What I'm most anxious about is getting back. Have we any chance?"

Arthur nodded emphatically.

"I think so. I have a sort of idea as to the cause of our sinking into the Fourth Dimension, and when that is verified, a corrective can be looked for and applied."

"How long will that take?"

"Can't say," Arthur replied frankly. "I don't know what tools, what materials, or what workmen we have, and what's rather more to the point, I don't even know what work will have to be done. The pressing problem is food."

"Oh, bother the food," some one protested impatiently. "I don't care about myself. I can go hungry to-night. I want to get back to my family."

"That's all that really matters," a chorus of voices echoed.

"We'd better not bother about anything else unless we find we can't get back. Concentrate on getting back," one man stated more explicitly.

"Look here," said Arthur incisively. "You've a family, and so have a great many of the others in the tower, but your family and everybody else's family has got to wait. As an inside limit, we can hope to begin to work on the problem of getting back when we're sure there's nothing else going to happen. I tell you quite honestly that I think I know what is the direct cause of this catastrophe. And I'll tell you even more honestly that I think I'm the only man among us who can put this tower back where it started from. And I'll tell you most honestly of all that any attempt to meddle at this present time with the forces that let us down here will result in a catastrophe considerably greater than the one that happened to-day."

"Well, if you're sure—" some one began reluctantly.

"I am so sure that I'm going to keep to myself the

knowledge of what will start those forces to work again," Arthur said quietly. "I don't want any impatient meddling. If we start them too soon God only knows what will happen."

Organizing the Food Supply

VAN Deventer was eying Arthur Chamberlain keenly.

"It isn't a question of your wanting pay in exchange for your services in putting us back, is it?" he asked coolly.

Arthur turned and faced him. His face began to flush slowly. Van Deventer put up one hand.

"I beg your pardon. I see."

"We aren't settling the things we came here for," Estelle interrupted.

She had noted the threat of friction and hastened to put in a diversion. Arthur relaxed.

"I think that as a beginning," he suggested, "we'd better get sleeping arrangements completed. We can get everybody together somewhere, I dare say, and then secure volunteers for the work."

"Right." Van Deventer was anxious to make amends for his blunder of a moment before. "Shall I send the bank watchmen to go on each floor in turn and ask everybody to come down-stairs?"

"You might start them," Arthur said. "It will take a long time for every one to assemble."

Van Deventer spoke into the telephone on his desk. In a moment he hung up the receiver.

"They're on their way," he said.

Arthur was frowning to himself and scribbling in a note-book.

"Of course," he announced abstractedly, "the pressing

problem is food. We've quite a number of fishermen, and a few hunters. We've got to have a lot of food at once, and everything considered, I think we'd better count on the fishermen. At sunrise we'd better have some people begin to dig bait and wake our anglers. They'd better make their tackle to-night, don't you think?"

There was a general nod.

"We'll announce that, then. The fishermen will go to the river under guard of the men we have who can shoot. I think what Indians there are will be much too frightened to try to ambush any of us, but we'd better be on the safe side. They'll keep together and fish at nearly the same spot, with our hunters patrolling the woods behind them, taking pot-shots at game, if they see any. The fishermen should make more or less of a success, I think. The Indians weren't extensive fishers that I ever heard of, and the river ought fairly to swarm with fish."

He closed his note-book.

"How many weapons can we count on altogether?" Arthur asked Van Deventer.

"In the bank, about a dozen riot-guns and half a dozen repeating rifles. Elsewhere I don't know. Forty or fifty men said they had revolvers, though."

"We'll give revolvers to the men who go with the fishermen. The Indians haven't heard firearms and will run at the report, even if they dare attack our men."

"We can send out the gun-armed men as hunters," some one suggested, "and send gardeners with them to look for vegetables and such things."

"We'll have to take a sort of census, really," Arthur suggested, "finding what every one can do and getting him to do it."

"I never planned anything like this before," Van Deventer remarked, "and I never thought I should, but this is much more fun than running a bank."

Arthur smiled.

"Let's go and have our meeting," he said cheerfully.

But the meeting was a gloomy and despairing affair. Nearly every one had watched the sun set upon a strange, wild landscape. Hardly an individual among the whole two thousand of them had ever been out of sight of a house before in his or her life. To look out at a vast, untouched wilderness where hitherto they had seen the most highly civilized city on the globe would have been startling and depressing enough in itself, but to know that they were alone in a whole continent of savages and that there was not, indeed, in all the world a single community of people they could greet as brothers was terrifying.

Few of them thought so far, but there was actually—if Arthur's estimate of several thousand years' drop back through time was correct—there was actually no other group of English-speaking people in the world. The English language was yet to be invented. Even Rome, the synonym for antiquity of culture, might still be an obscure village inhabited by a band of tatterdemalions under the leadership of an upstart Romulus.

Soft in body as these people were, city-bred and unaccustomed to face other than the most conventionalized emergencies of life, they were terrified. Hardly one of them had even gone without a meal in all his life. To have the prospect of having to earn their food, not by the manipulation of figures in a book, or by expert juggling of profits and prices, but by literal wresting of that food from its source in the earth or stream was a really terrifying thing for them.

In addition, every one of them was bound to the life of modern times by a hundred ties. Many of them had families, a thousand years away. All had interests, engrossing interests, in modern New York.

One young man felt an anxiety that was really ludicrous because he had promised to take his sweetheart to the theater that night, and if he did not come she would be very angry. Another was to have been married in a week. Some of the people were, like Van Deventer and Arthur, so situated that they could view the episode as an adventure, or, like Estelle, who had no immediate fear because all her family was provided for without her help and lived far from New York, so they would not learn of the catastrophe for some time. Many, however, felt instant and pressing fear for the families whose expenses ran always so close to their incomes that the disappearance of the breadwinner for a week would mean actual want or debt. There are very many such families in New York.

The people, therefore, that gathered hopelessly at the call of Van Deventer's watchmen were dazed and spiritless. Their excitement after Arthur's first attempt to explain the situation to them had evaporated. They were no longer keyed up to a high pitch by the startling thing that had happened to them.

Nevertheless, although only half comprehending what had actually occurred, they began to realize what that occurrence meant. No matter where they might go over the whole face of the globe, they would always be aliens and strangers. If they had been carried away to some unknown shore, some wilderness far from their own land, they might have thought of building ships to return to their homes. They had seen New York vanish before their eyes, however. They had seen their civilization disappear while they watched.

They were in a barbarous world. There was not, for example, a single sulfur match on the whole earth except those in the runaway skyscraper.

A Food-Riot in the Building

ARTHUR and Van Deventer, in turn with the others of the cooler heads, thundered at the apathetic people, trying to waken them to the necessity for work. They showered promises of inevitable return to modern times, they pledged their honor to the belief that a way would ultimately be found by which they would all yet find themselves safely back home again.

The people, however, had seen New York disintegrate, and Arthur's explanation sounded like some wild dream of an imaginative novelist. Not one person in all the gathering could actually realize that his home might yet be waiting for him, though at the same time he felt a pathetic anxiety for the welfare of its inmates.

Every one was in a turmoil of contradictory beliefs. On the one hand they knew that all of New York could not be actually destroyed and replaced by a splendid forest in the space of a few hours, so the accident or catastrophe must have occurred to those in the tower, and on the other hand, they had seen all of New York vanish by bits and fragments, to be replaced by a smaller and dingier town, had beheld that replaced in turn, and at last had landed in the midst of this forest.

Every one, too, began to feel am unusual and uncomfortable sensation of hunger. It was a mild discomfort as yet, but few of them had experienced it before without an immediate prospect of assuaging the craving, and the knowledge that there was no food to be had somehow increased the desire for it. They were really in a pitiful state.

Van Deventer spoke encouragingly, and then asked for volunteers for immediate work. There was hardly any response. Every one seemed sunk in despondency. Arthur then began to talk straight from the shoulder and succeeded in rousing them a little, but every one was still rather too frightened to realize that work could help at all.

In desperation the dozen or so men who had gathered in Van Deventer's office went about among the gathering and simply selected men at random, ordering them to follow and begin work. This began to awaken the crowd, but they wakened to fear rather than resolution. They were city-bred, and unaccustomed to face the unusual or the alarming.

Arthur noted the new restlessness, but attributed it to growing uneasiness rather than selfish panic. He was rather pleased that they were outgrowing their apathy. When the meeting had come to an end he felt satisfied that by morning the latent resolution among the people would have crystallized and they would be ready to work earnestly and intelligently on whatever tasks they were directed to undertake.

He returned to the ground floor of the building feeling much more hopeful than before. Two thousand people all earnestly working for one end are hard to down even when faced with such a task as confronted the inhabitants of the runaway skyscraper. Even if they were never able to return to modern times they would still be able to form a community that might do much to hasten the development of civilization in other parts of the world.

His hope received a rude shock when he reached the great hallway on the lower floor. There was a fruit and confectionery stand here, and as Arthur arrived at the spot, he saw a surging mass of men about it. The keeper of the stand looked frightened, but was selling off his stock as fast as he could make change. Arthur forced his way to the counter.

"Here," he said sharply to the keeper of the stand, "stop selling this stuff. It's got to be held until we can dole it out where it's needed."

"I—I can't help myself," the keeper said. "They're takin' it anyway."

"Get back there," Arthur cried to the crowd. "Do you call this decent, trying to get more than your share of this stuff? You'll get your portion to-morrow. It is going to be divided up."

"Go to hell!" some one panted. "You c'n starve if you want to, but I'm goin' to look out f'r myself."

The men were not really starving, but had been put into a panic by the plain speeches of Arthur and his helpers, and were seizing what edibles they could lay hands upon in preparation for the hunger they had been warned to expect.

Arthur pushed against the mob, trying to thrust them away from the counter, but his very effort intensified their panic. There was a quick surge and a crash. The glass front of the showcase broke in.

In a flash of rage Arthur struck out viciously. The crowd paid not the slightest attention to him, however. Every man was too panic-stricken, and too intent on getting some of this food before it was all gone to bother with him.

Arthur was simply crushed back by the bodies of the forty or fifty men. In a moment he found himself alone amid the wreckage of the stand, with the keeper wringing his hands over the remnants of his goods.

Van Deventer ran down the stairs.

"What's the matter?" he demanded as he saw Arthur nursing a bleeding hand cut on the broken glass of the showcase.

"Bolsheviki!" answered Arthur with a grim smile. "We woke up some of the crowd too successfully. They got panic-stricken and started to buy out this stuff here. I tried to stop them, and you see what happened. We'd better look to the restaurant, though I doubt if they'll try anything else just now."

He followed Van Deventer up to the restaurant floor. There were picked men before the door, but just as Arthur and the bank president appeared two or three white-faced men went up to the guards and started low-voiced conversations.

Arthur reached the spot in time to forestall bribery.

Arthur collared one man, Van Deventer another, and in a moment the two were sent reeling down the hallway.

"Some fools have got panic-stricken!" Van Deventer explained to the men before the doors in a casual voice, though he was breathing heavily from the unaccustomed exertion. "They've smashed up the fruit-stand on the ground floor and stolen the contents. It's nothing but blue funk! Only, if any of them start to gather around here, hit them first and talk it over afterward. You'll do that?"

"We will!" the men said heartily.

"Shall we use our guns?" asked another hopefully.

Van Deventer grinned.

"No," he replied, "we haven't any excuse for that yet. But you might shoot at the ceiling, if they get excited. They're just frightened!"

He took Arthur's arm, and the two walked toward the stairway again.

"Chamberlain," he said happily, "tell me why I've never had as much fun as this before!"

Arthur smiled a bit wearily.

"I'm glad you're enjoying yourself!" he said. "I'm not.

I'm going outside and walk around. I want to see if any cracks have appeared in the earth anywhere. It's dark, and I'll borrow a lantern down in the fire-room, but I want to find out if there are any more developments in the condition of the building."

Theorizing On the Strange Occurrence

DESPITE his preoccupation with his errand, which was to find if there were other signs of the continued activity of the strange forces that had lowered the tower through the Fourth Dimension into the dim and unrecorded years of aboriginal America, Arthur could not escape the fascination of the sight that met his eyes. A bright moon shone overhead and silvered the white sides of the tower, while the brightly-lighted windows of the offices within glittered like jewels set into the shining shaft.

From his position on the ground he looked into the dimness of the forest on all sides. Black obscurity had gathered beneath the dark masses of moonlit foliage. The tiny birch-bark teepees of the now deserted Indian village glowed palely. Above, the stars looked calmly down at the accusing finger of the tower pointing upward, as if in reproach at their indifference to the savagery that reigned over the whole earth.

Like a fairy tower of jewels the building rose. Alone among a wilderness of trees and streams it towered in a strange beauty: moonlit to silver, lighted from within to a mass of brilliant gems, it stood serenely still.

Arthur, carrying his futile lantern about its base, felt his own insignificance as never before. He wondered what the Indians must think. He knew there must be hundreds of eyes fixed upon the strange sight—fixed in awe-stricken terror or superstitious reverence upon this unearthly visitor to their hunting grounds.

A tiny figure, dwarfed by the building whose base he skirted, Arthur moved slowly about the vast pile. The earth seemed not to have been affected by the vast weight of the tower.

Arthur knew, however, that long concrete piles reached far down to bedrock. It was these piles that had sunk into the Fourth Dimension, carrying the building with them.

Arthur had followed the plans with great interest when the Metropolitan was constructed. It was an engineering feat, and in the engineering periodicals, whose study was a part of Arthur's business, great space had been given to the building and the methods of its construction.

While examining the earth carefully he went over his theory of the cause for the catastrophe. The whole structure must have sunk at the same time, or it, too, would have disintegrated, as the other buildings had appeared to disintegrate. Mentally, Arthur likened the submergence of the tower in the oceans of time to an elevator sinking past the different floors of an office building. All about the building the other sky-scrapers of New York had seemed to vanish. In an elevator, the floors one passes seem to rise upward.

Carrying out the analogy to its logical end, Arthur reasoned that the building itself had no more cause to disintegrate, as the buildings it passed seemed to disintegrate, than the elevator in the office building would have cause to rise because its surroundings seemed to rise.

Within the building, he knew, there were strange stirrings of emotions. Queer currents of panic were running about, throwing the people to and fro as leaves are thrown about by a current of wind. Yet, underneath all those undercurrents of fear, was a rapidly growing resolution, strengthened by an increasing knowledge of the need to work.

Men were busy even then shifting all possible comfortable furniture to a single story for the women in the building to occupy. The men would sleep on the floor for the present. Beds of boughs could be improvised on the morrow. At sunrise on the following morning many men would go to the streams to fish, guarded by other men. All would be frightened, no doubt, but there would be a grim resolution underneath the fear. Other men would wander about to hunt.

There was little likelihood of Indians approaching for some days, at least, but when they did come Arthur meant to avoid hostilities by all possible means. The Indians would be fearful of their strange visitors, and it should not be difficult to convince them that friendliness was safest, even if they displayed unfriendly desires.

The pressing problem was food. There were two thousand people in the building, soft-bodied and city-bred. They were unaccustomed to hardship, and could not endure what more primitive people would hardly have noticed.

They must be fed, but first they must be taught to feed themselves. The fishermen would help, but Arthur could only hope that they would prove equal to the occasion. He did not know what to expect from them. From the hunters he expected but little. The Indians were wary hunters, and game would be shy if not scarce.

The great cloud of birds he had seen at sunset was a hopeful sign. Arthur vaguely remembered stories of great flocks of wood-pigeons which had been exterminated, as the buffalo was exterminated. As he considered the remembrance became more clear.

They had flown in huge flocks which nearly darkened the

sky. As late as the forties of the nineteenth century they had been an important article of food, and had glutted the market at certain seasons of the year.

Estelle had said the birds he had seen at sunset were pigeons. Perhaps this was one of the great flocks. If it were really so, the food problem would be much lessened, provided a way could be found to secure them. The ammunition in the tower was very limited, and a shell could not be found for every bird that was needed, nor even for every three or four. Great traps must be devised, or bird-lime might possibly be produced. Arthur made a mental note to ask Estelle if she knew anything of bird-lime.

A vague, humming roar, altering in pitch, came to his ears. He listened for some time before he identified it as the sound of the wind playing upon the irregular surfaces of the tower. In the city the sound was drowned by the multitude of other noises, but here Arthur could hear it plainly.

He listened a moment, and became surprised at the number of night noises he could hear. In New York he had closed his ears to incidental sounds from sheer self-protection. Somewhere he heard the ripple of a little spring. As the idea of a spring came into his mind, he remembered Estelle's description of the deep-toned roar she had heard.

He put his hand on the cold stone of the building. There was still a vibrant quivering of the rock. It was weaker than before, but was still noticeable.

He drew back from the rock and looked up into the sky. It seemed to blaze with stars, far more stars than Arthur had ever seen in the city, and more than he had dreamed existed.

As he looked, however, a cloud seemed to film a portion of the heavens. The stars still showed through it, but they twinkled in a peculiar fashion that Arthur could not understand.

He watched in growing perplexity. The cloud moved very swiftly. Thin as it seemed to be, it should have been silvery from the moonlight, but the sky was noticeably darker where it moved. It advanced toward the tower and seemed to obscure the upper portion. A confused motion became visible among its parts. Wisps of it whirled away from the brilliantly lighted tower, and then returned swiftly toward it.

Arthur heard a faint tinkle, then a musical scraping, which became louder. A faint scream sounded, then another. The tinkle developed into the sound made by breaking glass, and the scraping sound became that of the broken fragments as they rubbed against the sides of the tower in their fall.

The scream came again. It was the frightened cry of a woman. A soft body struck the earth not ten feet from where Arthur stood, then another, and another.

Arthur and Estelle in Conference Again

ARTHUR urged the elevator boy to greater speed. They were speeding up the shaft as rapidly as possible, but it was not fast enough. When they at last reached the height at which the excitement seemed to be centered, the car was stopped with a jerk and Arthur dashed down the hall.

Half a dozen frightened stenographers stood there, huddled together.

"What's the matter?" Arthur demanded. Men were running, from the other floors to see what the trouble was.

"The—the windows broke, and—and something flew in at us!" one of them gasped. There was a crash inside the nearest office and the women screamed again.

Arthur drew a revolver from his pocket and advanced to

the door. He quickly threw it open, entered, and closed it behind him. Those left out in the hall waited tensely.

There was no sound. The women began to look even more frightened. The men shuffled their feet uneasily, and looked uncomfortably at one another. Van Deventer appeared on the scene, puffing a little from his haste.

The door opened again and Arthur came out. He was carrying something in his hands. He had put his revolver aside and looked somewhat foolish but very much delighted.

"The food question is settled," he said happily. "Look!"

He held out the object he carried. It was a bird, apparently a pigeon of some sort. It seemed to have been stunned, but as Arthur held it out it stirred, then struggled, and in a moment was flapping wildly in an attempt to escape.

"It's a wood-pigeon," said Arthur. "They must fly after dark sometimes. A big flock of them ran afoul of the tower and were dazed by the lights. They've broken a lot of windows, I dare say, but a great many of them ran into the stonework and were stunned. I was outside the tower, and when I came in they were dropping to the ground by hundreds. I didn't know what they were then, but if we wait twenty minutes or so I think we can go out and gather up our supper and breakfast and several other meals, all at once."

Estelle had appeared and now reached out her hands for the bird.

"I'll take care of this one," she said. "Wouldn't it be a good idea to see if there aren't some more stunned in the other offices?"

* * * * *

In half an hour the electric stoves of the restaurant were going at their full capacity. Men, cheerfully excited men now, were bringing in pigeons by armfuls, and other men were skinning them. There was no time to pluck them, though a great many of the women were busily engaged in that occupation.

As fast as the birds could be cooked they were served out to the impatient but much cheered castaways, and in a little while nearly every person in the place was walking casually about the halls with a roasted, broiled, or fried pigeon in his hands. The ovens were roasting pigeons, the frying-pans were frying them, and the broilers were loaded down with the small but tender birds.

The unexpected solution of the most pressing question cheered every one amazingly. Many people were still frightened, but less frightened than before. Worry for their families still oppressed a great many, but the removal of the fear of immediate hunger led them to believe that the other problems before them would be solved, too, and in as satisfactory a manner.

Arthur had returned to his office with four broiled pigeons in a sheet of wrapping-paper. As he somehow expected, Estelle was waiting there.

"Thought I'd bring lunch up," he announced. "Are you hungry?"

"Starving!" Estelle replied, and laughed.

The whole catastrophe began to become an adventure. She bit eagerly into a bird. Arthur began as hungrily on another. For some time neither spoke a word. At last, however, Arthur waved the leg of his second pigeon toward his desk.

"Look what we've got here!" he said.

Estelle nodded. The stunned pigeon Arthur had first picked up was tied by one foot to a paper-weight.

"I thought we might keep him for a souvenir," she

suggested.

"You seem pretty confident we'll get back, all right," Arthur observed. "It was surely lucky those blessed birds came along. They've heartened up the people wonderfully!"

"Oh, I knew you'd manage somehow!" said Estelle confidently.

"I manage?" Arthur repeated, smiling. "What have I done?"

"Why, you've done everything," affirmed Estelle stoutly. "You've told the people what to do from the very first, and you're going to get us back."

Arthur grinned, then suddenly his face grew a little more serious.

"I wish I were as sure as you are," he said. "I think we'll be all right, though, sooner or later."

"I'm sure of it," Estelle declared with conviction. "Why, you—"

"Why I?" asked Arthur again. He bent forward in his chair and fixed his eyes on Estelle's. She looked up, met his gaze, and stammered.

"You—you do things," she finished lamely.

"I'm tempted to do something now," Arthur said. "Look here, Miss Woodward, you've been in my employ for three or four months. In all that time I've never had anything but the most impersonal comments from you. Why the sudden change?"

The twinkle in his eyes robbed his words of any impertinence.

"Why, I really—I really suppose I never noticed you before," said Estelle.

"Please notice me hereafter," said Arthur. "I have been noticing you. I've been doing practically nothing else."

Estelle flushed again. She tried to meet Arthur's eyes and failed. She bit desperately into her pigeon drumstick, trying to think of something to say.

"When we get back," went on Arthur meditatively, "I'll have nothing to do—no work or anything. I'll be broke and out of a job."

Estelle shook her head emphatically. Arthur paid no attention.

"Estelle," he said, smiling, "would you like to be out of a job with me?"

Estelle turned crimson.

"I'm not very successful," Arthur went on soberly. "I'm afraid I wouldn't make a very good husband, I'm rather worthless and lazy!"

"You aren't," broke in Estelle; "you're—you're—"

Arthur reached over and took her by the shoulders.

"What?" he demanded.

She would not look at him, but she did not draw away. He held her from him for a moment.

"What am I?" he demanded again. Somehow he found himself kissing the tips of her ears. Her face was buried against his shoulder.

"What am I?" he repeated sternly.

Her voice was muffled by his coat.

"You're—you're dear!" she said.

There was an interlude of about a minute and a half, then she pushed him away from her.

"Don't!" she said breathlessly. "Please don't!"

"Aren't you going to marry me?" he demanded.

Still crimson, she nodded shyly. He kissed her again.

"Please don't!" she protested.

She fondled the lapels of his coat, quite content to have

his arms about her.

"Why mayn't I kiss you if you're going to marry me?" Arthur demanded.

She looked up at him with an air of demure primness.

"You—you've been eating pigeon," she told him in mock gravity, "and—and your mouth is greasy!"

A Geyser Effects a Happy Return

IT was two weeks later. Estelle looked out over the now familiar wild landscape. It was much the same when she looked far away, but near by there were great changes.

A cleared trail led through the woods to the waterfront, and a raft of logs extended out into the river for hundreds of feet. Both sides of the raft were lined with busy fishermen—men and women, too. A little to the north of the base of the building a huge mound of earth smoked sullenly. The coal in the cellar had given out and charcoal had been found to be the best substitute they could improvise. The mound was where the charcoal was made.

It was heart-breaking work to keep the fires going with charcoal, because it burned so rapidly in the powerful draft of the furnaces, but the original fire-room gang had been recruited to several times its original number from among the towerites, and the work was divided until it did not seem hard.

As Estelle looked down two tiny figures sauntered across the clearing from the woods with a heavy animal slung between them. One of them was using a gun as a walking-stick. Estelle saw the flash of the sun on its polished metal barrel.

There were a number of Indians in the clearing, watching with wide-open eyes the activities of the whites. Dozens of birch-bark canoes dotted the Hudson, each with its load of fishermen, industriously working for the white people. It had been hard to overcome the fear in the Indians, and they still paid superstitious reverence to the whites, but fair dealings, coupled with a constant readiness to defend themselves, had enabled Arthur to institute a system of trading for food that had so far proved satisfactory.

The whites had found spare electric-light bulbs valuable currency in dealing with the redmen. Picture-wire, too, was highly prized. There was not a picture left hanging in any of the offices. Metal paper-knives bought huge quantities of provisions from the eager Indian traders, and the story was current in the tower that Arthur had received eight canoe-loads of corn and vegetables in exchange for a broken-down typewriter. No one could guess what the savages wanted with the typewriter, but they had carted it away triumphantly.

Estelle smiled tenderly to herself as she remembered how Arthur had been the leading spirit in all the numberless enterprises in which the castaways had been forced to engage. He would come to her in a spare ten minutes, and tell her how everything was going. He seemed curiously boylike in those moments.

Sometimes he would come straight from the fire-room—he insisted on taking part in all the more arduous duties—having hastily cleaned himself for her inspection, snatch a hurried kiss, and then go off, laughing, to help chop down trees for the long fishing-raft. He had told them how to make charcoal, had taken a leading part in establishing and maintaining friendly relations with the Indians, and was now down in the deepest sub-basement, working with a gang of volunteers to try to put the building back where it belonged.

Estelle had said, after the collapse of the flooring in the board-room, that she heard a sound like the rushing of waters. Arthur, on examining the floor where the safe-deposit vault stood, found it had risen an inch. On these facts he had built up his theory. The building, like all modern sky-scrapers, rested on concrete piles extending down to bedrock. In the center of one of those piles there was a hollow tube originally intended to serve as an artesian well. The flow had been insufficient and the well had been stopped up.

Arthur, of course, as an engineer, had studied the construction of the building with great care, and happened to remember that this partly hollow pile was the one nearest the safe-deposit vault. The collapse of the board-room floor had suggested that some change had happened in the building itself, and that was found when he saw that the deposit-vault had actually risen an inch.

He at once connected the rise in the flooring above the hollow pile with the pipe in the pile. Estelle had heard liquid sounds. Evidently water had been forced into the hollow artesian pipe under an unthinkable pressure when the catastrophe occurred.

From the rumbling and the suddenness of the whole catastrophe a volcanic or seismic disturbance was evident. The connection of volcanic or seismic action with a flow of water suggested a geyser or a hot spring of some sort, probably a spring which had broken through its normal confines some time before, but whose pressure had been sufficient to prevent the accident until the failure of its flow.

When the flow ceased the building sank rapidly. For the fact that this "sinking" was in the fourth direction—the Fourth Dimension—Arthur had no explanation. He simply knew that in some mysterious way an outlet for the pressure had developed in that fashion, and that the tower had followed the spring in its fall through time.

The sole apparent change in the building had occurred

above the one hollow concrete pile, which seemed to indicate that if access were to be had to the mysterious, and so far only assumed spring, it must be through that pile. While the vault retained its abnormal elevation, Arthur believed that there was still water at an immense and incalculable pressure in the pipe. He dared not attempt to tap the pipe until the pressure had abated.

At the end of a week he found the vault slowly settling back into place. When its return to the normal was complete he dared begin boring a hole to reach the hollow tube in the concrete pile.

As he suspected, he found water in the pile—water whose sulfurous and mineral nature confirmed his belief that a geyser reaching deep into the bosom of the earth, as well as far back in the realms of time, was at the bottom of the extraordinary jaunt of the tower.

Geysers were still far from satisfactory things to explain. There are many of their vagaries which we cannot understand at all. We do know a few things which affect them, and one thing is that "soaping" them will stimulate their flow in an extraordinary manner.

Arthur proposed to "soap" this mysterious geyser when the renewal of its flow should lift the runaway sky-scraper back to the epoch from which the failure of the flow had caused it to fall.

He made his preparations with great care. He confidently expected his plan to work, and to see the sky-scraper once more towering over mid-town New York as was its wont, but he did not allow the fishermen and hunters to relax their efforts on that account. They labored as before, while deep down in the sub-basement of the colossal building Arthur and his volunteers toiled mightily.

They had to bore through the concrete pile until they reached the hollow within it. Then, when the evidence gained from the water in the pipe had confirmed his surmises, they had to prepare their "charge" of soapy liquids by which the geyser was to be stirred to renewed activity.

Great quantities of the soap used by the scrubwomen in scrubbing down the floors was boiled with water until a sirupy mess was evolved. Means had then to be provided by which this could be quickly introduced into the hollow pile, the hole then closed, and then braced to withstand a pressure unparalleled in hydraulic science. Arthur believed that from the hollow pile the soapy liquid would find its way to the geyser proper, where it would take effect in stimulating the lessened flow to its former proportions. When that took place he believed that the building would return as swiftly and as surely as it had left them to normal, modern times.

The telephone rang in his office, and Estelle answered it. Arthur was on the wire. A signal was being hung out for all the castaway to return to the building from their several occupations. They were about to soap the geyser.

Did Estelle want to come down and watch? She did! She stood in the main hallway as the excited and hopeful people trooped in. When the last was inside the doors were firmly closed. The few friendly Indians outside stared perplexedly at the mysterious white strangers.

The whites, laughing excitedly, began to wave to the Indians. Their leave-taking was premature.

Estelle took her way down into the cellar. Arthur was awaiting her arrival. Van Deventer stood near, with the grinning, grimy members of Arthur's volunteer work gang. The massive concrete pile stood in the center of the cellar. A big steam-boiler was coupled to a tiny pipe that led into the heart of the mass of concrete. Arthur was going to force the soapy liquid into the hollow pile by steam.

At a signal steam began to hiss in the boiler. Live steam from the fire-room forced the soapy sirup out of the boiler, through the small iron pipe, into the hollow that led to the geyser far underground. Six thousand gallons in all were forced into the opening in a space of three minutes.

Arthur's grimy gang began to work with desperate haste. Quickly they withdrew the iron pipe and inserted a long steel plug, painfully beaten from a bar of solid metal. Then, girding the colossal concrete pile, ring after ring of metal was slipped on, to hold the plug in place.

The last of the safeguards was hardly fastened firmly when Estelle listened intently.

"I hear a rumbling!" she said quietly.

Arthur reached forward and put his hand on the mass of concrete.

"It is quivering!" he reported as quietly. "I think we'll be on our way in a very little while."

The group broke for the stairs, to watch the panorama as the runaway sky-scraper made its way back through the thousands of years to the times that had built it for a monument to modern commerce.

Arthur and Estelle went high up in the tower. From the window of Arthur's office they looked eagerly, and felt the slight quiver as the tower got under way. Estelle looked up at the sun, and saw it mend its pace toward the west.

Night fell. The evening sounds became high-pitched and shrill, then seemed to cease altogether.

In a very little while there was light again, and the sun was speeding across the sky. It sank hastily, and returned almost immediately, *via* the east. Its pace became a breakneck rush.

Down behind the hills and up in the east. Down in the west, up in the east. Down and up— The flickering began. The race back toward modern times had started.

Arthur and Estelle stood at the window and looked out as the sun rushed more and more rapidly across the sky until it became but a streak of light, shifting first to the right and then to the left as the seasons passed in their turn.

With Arthur's arms about her shoulders, Estelle stared out across the unbelievable landscape, while the nights and days, the winters and summers, and the storms and calms of a thousand years swept past them into the irrevocable past.

Presently Arthur drew her to him and kissed her. While he kissed her, so swiftly did the days and years flee by, three generations were born, grew and begot children, and died again!

Estelle, held fast in Arthur's arms, thought nothing of such trivial things. She put her arms about his neck and kissed him, while the years passed them unheeded.

*****

Of course you know that the building landed safely, in the exact hour, minute, and second from which it started, so that when the frightened and excited people poured out of it to stand in Madison Square and feel that the world was once more right side up, their hilarious and incomprehensible conduct made such of the world as was passing by think a contagious madness had broken out.

Days passed before the story of the two thousand was believed, but at last it was accepted as truth, and eminent scientists studied the matter exhaustively.

There has been one rather queer result of the journey of the runaway sky-scraper. A certain Isidore Eckstein, a dealer in jewelry novelties, whose office was in the tower when it disappeared into the past, has entered suit in the courts of the United States against all the holders of land on Manhattan Island. It seems that during the two weeks in which the tower rested in the wilderness he traded independently with one of the Indian chiefs, and in exchange for two near-pearl necklaces, sixteen finger-rings, and one dollar in money, received a title-deed to the entire island.—He claims that his deed is a conveyance made previous to all other sales whatever.

Strictly speaking, he is undoubtedly right, as his deed was signed before the discovery of America. The courts, however, are deliberating the question with a great deal of perplexity.

Eckstein is quite confident that in the end his claim will be allowed and he will be admitted as the sole owner of real-estate on Manhattan Island, with all occupiers of buildings and territory paying him ground rent at a rate he will fix himself. In the mean time, though the foundations are being reinforced so the catastrophe cannot occur again, his entire office is packed full of articles suitable for trading with the Indians. If the tower makes another trip back through time, Eckstein hopes to become a landholder of some importance.

No less than eighty-seven books have been written by members of the memorable two thousand in description of their trip to the hinterland of time, but Arthur, who could write more intelligently about the matter than any one else, is so extremely busy that he cannot bother with such things. He has two very important matters to look after. One is, of course, the reenforcement of the foundations of the building so that a repetition of the catastrophe cannot occur, and the other is to convince his wife—who is Estelle, naturally—that she is the most adorable person in the universe. He finds the latter task the more difficult, because she insists that *he* is the most adorable person—

Made in the USA
Middletown, DE
06 December 2017